Fearsome's Hero

by Dona Schenker

Alfred A. Knopf
New York

6077986

This is a work of fiction. While Matagorda Island is an actual place, all names, characters, situations, incidents, and dialogues contained in this book are wholly fictional.

THIS IS A BORZOI BOOK PUBLISHED BY ALFRED A. KNOPF, INC.

Text copyright © 1994 by Dona Schenker
Cover art copyright © 1994 by Dan Andreasen

Library of Congress Cataloging-in-Publication Data

Schenker, Dona
Fearsome's Hero / by Dona Schenker
p.   cm.
Summary: Tully, who lives on a Texas ranch, faces trouble when Honey, the bossiest girl in the sixth grade and his former tormentor, decides that he is her hero.
ISBN 0-679-85424-X (trade)
[1. Schools—Fiction. 2. Ranch life—Texas—Fiction.
3. Texas—Fiction.] I. Title.
PZ7.S34356Fe   1994
[Fic]—dc20   93-8601

Manufactured in the United States of America
10 9 8 7 6 5 4 3 2 1

For Cecil
I love you

1

Tully Webster blinked at the cardboard sign hanging by a wire from the old canvas tent. KOTCHER'S YOU CAN BELIEVE IT OR NOT MUSEUM—I DON'T CARE. NO REFUNDS, it said.

He took a step back and shook his head. "I'm not goin' in there."

"Come on, Tully," R.J. Loomis said. "She's got that horny toad named Rip that smokes real cigarettes and a pair of fighting tarantulas that tear each other's legs off. It's only a quarter, too."

"She'd tear my legs off for a quarter," Tully said.

"Maybe she don't hate you anymore. Maybe she's found a brand-new person over the summer to pick on."

Tully shook his head. "Uh-uh. I'm stayin' away from her as long as I can. You go on in. I'll wait out here."

3

R.J. shrugged and disappeared inside the tent.

Tully stood behind a palm tree, facing the wharf. He held a bag full of school supplies, and he chewed at his lower lip. He'd tried to forget about Honey Kotcher all summer. Now it was the Saturday before school started again. Here she was, not ten feet away. Just thinking about her made him feel as if bugs were crawling down his neck.

It had all started last year, in fifth grade, when he accidentally tripped her on the playground during lunch. She snapped one of her famous headlocks on him and wiped the mustard from his bologna sandwich all over his face.

When she loosened her grip, dropping him to the ground with a thud, he made the mistake of letting her see him cry. She nicknamed him "Boo Hoo" on the spot, calling him "Boo" for short ever after.

"Boo!" Honey would yell when she leapt out of the shadows in the hall at school, making him jump.

"Oh, Boo Hoo," she'd call, hands on her hips, when he walked in the door every morning.

Probably she could smell fear the way a mean dog could.

"Leave me alone," he'd say. She'd grab his arm so tight he could feel her fingers pinching the bone, and look at him with eyes mean and narrow as a cat's under her freckled eyelids, standing strong and solid as a house. She had a way of swinging her head kind of slow and fierce, ending the swing with Tully impaled on the end of her glare. "Make me," she'd say.

The other kids mostly looked at him with sympathy and relief that she was after him that year and not them.

"Toodle-oo, Boo Hoo," she'd yell after him when he walked down the road toward the ranch after school.

"You should sock the nose off her fat freckled face," R.J. would urge.

"You're not supposed to hit a girl," Tully would say. "Besides, she's a lot bigger'n me. She'd kill me dead."

By the end of the school year he'd chewed his fingernails to nubbins and offered his mother every argument for home schooling he could think of.

He and R.J. had nicknamed her "Fearsome," yet even now R.J. was inside the tent watching her show. Tully looked at the neatly printed sign. Each of the letters was a different color. Underneath, she'd painted a fierce-looking horned toad and a black tarantula with red eyes. Honey could sure paint, Tully had to admit.

Chickens cackled inside the tent. Tully spied a low hole in the canvas and crept over to look through it.

A knot of small children were huddled together inside. Honey stood behind a table that held an aluminum-foil stage.

"Kotcher's famous dancing chickens," Honey announced. She plopped two red hens down on the little stage.

Tully knew for an absolute concrete fact that there was a hot plate underneath the foil. No wonder the poor chickens hopped from foot to foot, cackling all the while! It was the oldest trick in the book. But dang if it didn't look like they were really dancing. Tully counted fourteen heads inside the tent. She was probably making a fortune.

Honey glanced in Tully's direction. Tully drew back. If she caught him spying, he'd be dead.

From across the clearing behind him, a truck backfired. Mr. Diddums, the game warden, pulled into a parking space in front of the Island Store and went inside. His pickup shimmered in the heat. How did Diddums sneak up on poachers with a truck that made so much noise?

Loud shrieking came from the tent, and Tully crept back to the hole. Honey dangled hissing lizards from strings tied around their necks. She swooped the lizards back and forth over her audience's heads.

"Snatched back from the beginning of time . . . baby dinosaurs!" Honey brayed. Her face was red and splotched in the heat, like a strawberry pudding.

One of the hissing lizards got caught in Millie Loomis's hair. Millie screamed and Honey yanked the lizard back. It hissed and made a little barking sound.

Dang, what are those things? Tully squinted to see better.

Mr. Diddums and Mr. Filbert, the store owner, came out on the porch and stood under the wooden awning to talk. For a fleeting moment, Tully was embarrassed to be seen spying, but he had to know what kind of lizards Honey had.

Honey was really carried away now, swinging the lizards back and forth, encouraged by the shrieks. One swooped in an arc close to the hole, and Tully knew instantly that they weren't just lizards.

He glanced behind him. Mr. Diddums and Mr. Filbert were staring intently at the tent. "What's all the yelling about?" Diddums said.

He was going to catch Honey for sure, Tully thought. On impulse, Tully rushed to the back of the tent, lifted the flap up, and saw the back of Honey's legs.

"Honey," he whispered. "Honey!"

"What are *you* doing here?" Honey put her

face down to his, thrusting it at him like a shaken fist.

Just seeing her this close made Tully's voice shake. She had coppery red hair that stood out in the heat like corkscrews, and orange eyebrows and eyelashes. Maybe he should just say, "Never mind," and run off. Yet Tully felt like a toy that had been wound up with a key and couldn't stop.

"Those aren't dinosaurs, Honey, they're baby alligators." Tully tried to whisper, but his throat was dry and it came out loud.

"Read the sign, Boo Hoo. You can believe it or not, *I* don't care. You didn't even pay."

"Thing is, Honey, the game warden's about thirty feet away." Tully talked faster now; if he slowed down, he might lose his nerve. "Alligators are protected in Texas. If he catches you with them, you'll get a whopping big fine or you might even go to jail."

Honey put one hand on her hip. She still held the alligators aloft by strings in her other hand. They pawed the air and hissed like baby kittens. Tully peered around the side of the tent. Diddums and Filbert, puzzled looks on their faces, were walking slowly through the clearing toward the tent.

"They're coming," Tully said.

Honey grabbed a cardboard box and dropped the baby alligators inside, strings and all. She shoved the box into Tully's stomach.

"Take them behind the bait stand and wait for me there." She jerked the tent flap down.

Tully bolted down the length of the pier and dashed behind the bait stand, out of sight. He waited, the box in his arms, and panted in the thick heavy air that was humming with flies. One lit down on his hand and diddled its feet together. A baby alligator crawled out of the box and scampered across the pier. Tully snatched it up by the tail. It squirmed around and bit his finger, drawing blood.

"Dang!" He threw it back in the box and sucked his finger. What am I doing here with a box full of alligators? There had to be twenty or thirty of the hissing varmints. He tried to count them, but they crawled all over each other and he soon lost count.

What if the game warden had seen him running down the pier and decided to follow him? *He* could be thrown in jail instead of Honey. Worse still, they could be thrown in jail together, in the same cell. He heard heavy footsteps and peeked around the bait stand to look, expecting to see Diddums carrying handcuffs.

2

Instead of Diddums, Honey appeared. The sight of her, all big and red-faced and sweaty, didn't make Tully feel much better. He handed her the box.

"You really saved my butt, Tully," Honey said, looming above him.

Would she leave him alone now? "Well . . . um . . . ," he said.

She looked at the alligators in the box and sort of smiled at Tully. "They were big old eggs in a nest when I found them in a hollow down at Pringle Pond this summer." Her green eyes, round as a rabbit's, were sparkling. "I took about twenty-five eggs from the nest and put them in this old rotten tree stump in my backyard. I covered them with sand and leaves and sticks, but then I forgot about them. One morning I went out to take the wash off the line, and there they were, standing up on all fours with their mouths open, hissing at me."

"Well," Tully said and cleared his throat. "They do look kind of like baby dinosaurs." He saw R.J. waiting for him at the end of the pier.

"Guess I'll have to let 'em go tomorrow," Honey said. "They've sure been a lot of company."

That seemed to use up all their topics of conversation. When Tully edged by her on the dock, she clamped a meaty hand on his shoulder, making him jump. That's when he noticed a purplish-yellow bruise on her arm. She'd probably gotten it in a fight with someone as tough as she was.

"Thanks a lot, Tully. That's about the nicest thing anyone's ever done for me. See you Monday."

"Sure," Tully said. "Monday."

He ran down the pier and kept running, right past R.J., as fast as he could. R.J. finally caught up with him at the edge of the village.

"Why didn't you let the game warden get

ol' Fearsome?" R.J. asked. "If Diddums had nabbed her, maybe she wouldn't be back in school this year."

Honey had never beat up on R.J., but Tully knew he had his own ax to grind with her. Last year when R.J. hadn't chosen her for his relay team, she had brought a mess of live crickets from the bait stand and snuck them into his lunch box. R.J. was sitting at the teacher's table when he opened the box full of swarming crickets. They hopped all over the cafeteria, chirping loudly. The teacher made him stay after lunch to catch them while everyone else went to recess.

"I don't know why I covered for her," Tully lied. "Maybe I felt sorry for her." R.J. had been his best friend for as long as he could remember, but Tully didn't want to talk or even think about Honey Kotcher.

"I like alligators," Tully added lamely. He had to get R.J. off this subject. "What are you doing the rest of the day?"

"You want to come to the station?" R.J. asked. "They're washing the boats this afternoon." R.J.'s father was a captain at the Coast

Guard station. They lived in a little house on the point, and all the ships passed right in front of their yard.

"Naw. I need to check on Risky. I'll see you Monday."

Tully took off running down the sandy road, the heavy sack slapping against his leg. He passed the wire fence and then the rock fence and finally stopped to catch his breath at the stone-arched gate to his family's ranch. On the arch over the gate was a wood sign in the shape of a tail with a diamond at the end. The words DIAMOND TAIL RANCH were burned into the oak. Tully climbed over the gate and headed toward the barn down a road lined with palm trees.

Lately, Tully was jumpy and anxious to get back home whenever he was gone for more than an hour. His mare, Risky, was due to foal anytime now, and he wanted to be there when it happened.

He walked though the passageway into the gloom of the barn. The smell of oats all around him mingled with the musty odor of rats and mice.

Risky, her belly big as a barrel, dozed in her box stall at the end of the barn, her head hanging to her knees. Tully picked up a pulling comb and brushed her mane. Her ears went back, and she reached around to bite his arm, but he popped her head with his elbow.

"You're meaner'n a rattlesnake in a hot skillet, Risky," he said.

It had been true since the day she'd come to the Diamond Tail two years ago. Bigun Bailey, the ranch foreman, had traded a bull for her because she was supposed to be the best cutting horse—or cattle herder—on Matagorda Island. The day they unloaded her, she'd backed out of the trailer, her tail in the air and her ears almost crossed.

"Whoa," Bigun said. "Looks like the devil is a-loose."

Bigun was a tall, heavy-boned, biscuit-bodied man. He'd been with the Diamond Tail since Tully's father was killed in a truck accident while Tully was still a baby. Tully had always looked on Bigun as a father.

Bigun had known right away that Risky was an outlaw, but with her glossy sorrel coat and stocking legs, she was the most wonderful horse Tully had ever seen.

When Bigun and some of the hands tried to use her, they always ended up dumped on the ground, swearing at her. One afternoon when they were moving cattle from the sand dunes to the beach, she pitched Bigun again. He hit the wet sand so hard the stirrups popped over the top of the saddle.

Tully and Red, one of the cowboys, were giggling and snickering from a safe distance, until Bigun drew his rifle from behind his saddle. While they gaped in stunned silence, the huge old man raised the gun and aimed it at Risky's head.

Red got off his horse and tapped Bigun on the shoulder. "Bigun, maybe we better think this thing over. She's a dirty, human-hating cuss, and something has got to be done about her. But if you shoot her here, we're going to have to drag her. I know you're not about to leave no dead horse lying on the beach."

Bigun lowered the rifle and looked at Tully. "Son, you lead this fool horse back to the ranch. I'll finish up here with yours."

Tully waited until they were out of sight before he tried to mount Risky. He wanted to ride her even if she did rear up or pitch him on his backside. When he started to mount, Risky jerked her head and snorted. He put his foot in the stirrup and swung up. The horse humped her back and crab-stepped a little, but that was all. For some reason, if only because he was no heavier than a billy goat, she tolerated him. From that day on, she'd been his.

She would still fight with other horses, and she'd pitch and bite and buck, but she was so pretty and smart that her behavior hardly bothered Tully. In fact, her rebellious nature was a challenge, and Tully secretly knew it was one of the reasons he loved her so much. Besides, when Risky wasn't pitching fits, she was the best cutting horse he'd ever been on.

And anyway right now, Risky was too big and tired and clumsy to do much damage.

Bigun came out of the feed room with Tully's mother. They studied Risky in her stall.

"You're a fool for that horse, Tully," his

mother finally said. "Have you gotten any of your chores done today?"

"Yes, ma'am," Tully said. "I cleaned the pens this morning, and I bought my school supplies in the village." He dug the change out of his pockets and handed over the coins.

Bigun rubbed the silvery stubble on his face. "What kind of a mother do you think this she-devil's going to make?"

"She'll be as good a mother as any," Tully said, and grinned. "It's you she don't like, Bigun."

"Let's just hope motherhood calms her down some," his mother said.

Tully brushed Risky's withers. She laid her ears back and gave the stall door a thumping kick.

"Hah," Bigun said. "She'll still be every bit as waspy as anything that ever walked on four legs and neighed."

Tully mucked out Risky's stall and made her a fresh bed of bright, long straw. He filled the grain box with oats. Tired and sweaty by the time he finished, he climbed up the chaff-dusted ladder into the barn loft to cool off.

The high loft doors were open. Tully sat with his back against a bale of hay, while Bigun and his mother talked on the front porch of the white ranch house. It was surrounded by big bearded palm trees and had pens and windmills beyond it. Cattle that appeared mouse-sized grazed in the distance on salt grass in the dunes, and a few stragglers wandered along the beach on the Gulf of Mexico side of the island. The lighthouse and the white-washed Coast Guard station were perched on the point; on clear days, it was possible to see all the way across the bay to Port Call, Texas, where Tully's daddy had been born and was buried.

A little to the east, the gray brick school-house squatted in the center of the village, looking like a toy that you could lift up and hurl out to sea. Tully wished he could. If this year was anything like last year, he didn't think he'd be able to take it.

Tully's father had died when he was so young that Tully had no memories of him.

Usually, since Bigun and Red were like family, he could go to them with his questions. But there were times when he couldn't talk to anyone. During these spells, Tully couldn't help thinking that a real father might have special words of advice that would make his problems disappear.

The reason he'd covered for Honey earlier made Tully feel ashamed. He'd sucked up to her so maybe—just maybe—she'd leave him alone. If somebody picked on you all the time, and that somebody had at least thirty pounds and four inches on you, how did you fight back? Especially if that somebody was a girl.

3

The first day of school was full of surprises. Honey Kotcher was the first person Tully saw when he walked into the sixth-grade classroom at Matagorda School, and she smiled at him.

"Hi, Tully," she said. She carried a box of African violets to the green metal teacher's desk at the head of the room. "Miss Whistler asked me to put these flowers on her desk."

Tully felt weak-kneed with relief. He'd expected her to jump out of the shadows and startle him or yell, "Hi, Boo Hoo!" in a voice dripping with sarcasm. Instead, she stood over him and grinned like a banshee.

"I took the alligators back to Pringle Pond yesterday and let 'em loose on the shore. You should have seen them run every which way. I hope they can find their mama." She swung her body so that her skirt swished against her legs. "Do you think she'll eat them?"

"Who?" Tully asked. He was having a hard

time concentrating on what she was saying. A friendly Honey puzzled him.

Honey frowned. "The mama alligator. Maybe she won't know they're hers, and she'll eat them."

"No," Tully said. "The bull alligator would be more likely to do that." He couldn't think of anything else to say. She stood there and stared at him.

Tully's eyes darted around the room, looking for familiar faces. Kids trickled through the door in their Sunday-school clothes. Tomorrow they'd have their blue jeans and T-shirts on, but the first day of school called for starched shirts and khaki slacks for the boys and dresses for the girls.

Honey took the pots of violets out of the box and arranged them on the surface of the desk. She usually wore shorts or blue jeans, but today even she had on a blue cotton dress and black patent shoes, and her red hair was pulled back into a ponytail. Her dress was too tight across her chest, and her shoes were so big that they slapped the floor when she walked. She was larger than anyone in the class, even John Ed Koontz, and he'd been held back a year.

R.J. staggered in, swaybacked beneath a load of books. His yellow hair was slicked back as if he'd plastered it with lard and run a rake through it.

"Save me a seat by you, Tully," R.J. called. "I'm helping Miss Whistler bring the books in."

Tully jumped at the opportunity to get away. "Here, I'll help you."

By the time Tully and R.J. had brought down another load of books, the bell had rung. The PA system crackled on. While the principal, Mr. Barnes, led the school in the Pledge of Allegiance, Tully scanned the room for seats. He had wanted to sit by the big windows, but there were only two seats left, one in the back and one in the first row by the wall, right next to Honey Kotcher.

"Take your seats, boys," Miss Whistler called from the rear of the room.

Honey yanked Tully's wrist and said, "Here, Tully. Sit across from me." She pushed him down into the scarred, initialed desk next to hers.

Tully felt trapped and helpless as R.J. went to the other empty seat. What's going on? he wondered.

Miss Whistler flipped the light switch off and on until all the talking stopped. She had wasp's-nest gray hair done up like a cow patty on top of her head, and her lips were bitten together in a straight line. She was so old that she'd taught Tully's father when he'd been in the sixth grade. At least, that's what Tully's mother told him. Miss Whistler used to be strict about talking in the classroom, but now she couldn't always hear what students were saying. It was said that she heard only every third word in a sentence.

"She may not hear so well anymore," Tully's mother had told him, "but don't you forget that she can see, and she's brisk as a sparrow."

Miss Whistler wrote her name on the board and took attendance from her roll book. Name tags were passed out, hall monitors were assigned, and the class voted R.J. fire marshal. The rest of the morning was taken up with trips to the school nurse, and there were endless forms to fill out.

"Class, let's put our school supplies away in our desks," Miss Whistler finally said, "and then, while I'm passing out the textbooks, I want you to write an essay about the highlight of your summer."

Sighing filled the room. No one wanted to write a dumb essay on the first day of school.

Tully described the day in July when he got up at four a.m. and helped Bigun and Red gather new calves that had been born in the spring. He drove them into pens, and Bigun and Red branded and dipped them. He would have liked to write about the day Risky had her foal, but it hadn't happened yet.

He glanced across at Honey. Her tongue was caught in the corner of her mouth, and her forehead was wrinkled with concentration. She wrote with the stub of a gnawed pencil, probably about the hissing alligators.

While the class worked, Miss Whistler shuffled through the aisles, distributing textbooks. John Ed Koontz finished his essay first, and she called on him to stand up and read it aloud to the class.

John Ed, his ears standing out like jug handles, peered at his paper. "I helped out on my dad's shrimp boat this summer. Mostly, I steered the boat while my dad trawled. When we finished catching the shrimp late in the afternoon, we took the boat across the bay to a dock at Port Call. My dad sells most of his catch to a restaurant over there."

John Ed cast a bashful look at the class before finishing. "The best time of day on the water is early in the morning before it gets real hot. When the sun comes up over the water, it reminds me of a big red cinnamon jawbreaker."

Ceroy Taylor snickered, then so did Tookie Filbert. Tookie was so busy being Ceroy's sidekick that he'd laugh if Ceroy announced his funeral.

"It matches your big ol' cinnamon red ears, John Ed," Honey Kotcher called.

John Ed was red from his thin neck up to his hairline. He pressed his hands to his ears and sat down.

Miss Whistler squinted at a name tag and called on Nell Bailey. "Nell's new here," Miss Whistler said. "See that you all make her feel welcome."

Nell had hay-colored hair to the middle of her back and a light sprinkling of freckles across her cheeks. Tully liked the way she looked.

"My family moved here from North Carolina in June," Nell read, "when my father got relocated to the Coast Guard station. I've lived in fourteen different states since I was born, but none of them was anything like this island. I don't like alligators and snakes, and I get scared at night when the loons call from Pringle Pond. They sound like women screaming for help."

Nell glanced up from her paper, blinked her big blue eyes, and swallowed hard. Tully felt sorry for her.

"Ninny-baby," Honey muttered.

Nell returned to her paper. "When it's hot,

we sleep on the roof, and I watch the beam from the lighthouse swing around in the dark. The ocean looks pretty at night. I guess the welcoming party for us at the Coast Guard station was the high point of my summer."

"Big deal." Honey blew into her fist, producing a rude honk.

Nell's face reddened, and she sat down.

Couldn't Honey ever leave people alone? It was hard enough to get up in the first place, particularly if you were new.

Most of the kids told familiar stories of life on the island. Everything on Matagorda revolved around the Coast Guard station, or around catching and selling fish, or raising cattle on the three island ranches. Carrie Ellis and Sissy West told about a trip across the bay on the ferry to shop at the mall in Port Call. Ceroy Taylor's father was the foreman at the Lazy Y Ranch, and Ceroy had gone clear to Prero, Texas, with him to bring back a bull. Tully felt a little jealous. Bigun had never taken him any farther than the loading docks at Port Call to pick up cattle or horses.

Tully was rethinking the high point of his

summer when Miss Whistler called on Honey. Honey stood by her seat and faced the class. She took a deep breath, and her broad shoulders rose and fell. "The high point of my summer came day before yesterday. It all started out as a plain ol' day, but by the end of it I knew that I had met my hero."

Ceroy snickered, and giggling broke out at the back of the room, where Carrie and Sissy and Tookie sat.

"Honey's got a hero?" Carrie whispered to Sissy.

"Who is it? Quasimodo?" Sissy whispered back.

Tully's face burned. How could Honey say something like that right out loud in front of the teacher and the whole class? Who in the world could be her hero?

Miss Whistler looked up sharply, puzzled about the noise in the room. There was cold fire in Honey's green eyes, and she glared at Carrie and Sissy and Ceroy. The room was quiet again.

She continued. "This is the nicest thing that's ever happened to me." With that, she gave Tully a look fraught with so much adoration that he paled and stared at her, slack-jawed.

Tully loosened his collar and swallowed. Is it me? he wondered. Is Honey Kotcher's hero *me?*

4

"That will be enough, Honey," Miss Whistler said.

With a crash, a window shattered over Rhoda Webb's head, sending glass flying over the front of the room. Something whizzed by Honey's ear and hit the wall above Tully's head with a whack.

Miss Whistler clapped her hands as a baseball rolled across the floor. "Quiet," she yelled over the clamor. "Quiet! Has anyone been injured?"

When she was sure that everyone was fine, she shuffled out of the room to investigate the source of the runaway ball. Tully ran to the windows with the rest of the class.

"Looks like Dane Dugan done stepped in it good this time," R.J. said. They watched the principal grab Dane, a seventh grader, by the belt and turkey-walk him off the playing field to the office.

Honey stood so close to Tully he could smell the strawberry jam she'd had for breakfast. "That baseball almost killed us," she whispered hoarsely, her eyes burning into him.

Tully had a weird feeling in his stomach. Honey had been nice to him all morning, even had him sit by her. She'd given him that goggle-eyed look when she read her essay, and now she was looking at him funny again, as if he was special to her.

"Tullis!" Miss Whistler called from the door.

"Yes, ma'am?" Tully answered.

"We're going to lunch early," Miss Whistler said. "I can't find the janitor anywhere. Please choose someone to help you sweep up the glass. Then you may join the rest of us in the cafeteria."

Honey's hand shot up, and she gave Tully a pleading look, but he looked past her to choose R.J.

The class filed out with their brown bags, and Miss Whistler gave Tully a broom and R.J. a dustpan before following the others.

"How's this been for an exciting first day of

school?" R.J. asked, his blue eyes bright as a barn cat's. "Miss Whistler can't hear much, which makes her the perfect teacher as far as I'm concerned, and old Dane Dugan's got himself in a heap of trouble. I can hardly wait to see what happens this afternoon."

R.J. sat down and pulled a banana out of his lunch bag as Tully swept shards of glass into a pile.

"R.J., I swear I think I'm Honey Kotcher's hero."

"Aw, go on, Tully. She hates your guts."

"She did until I opened my mouth and told her Diddums was going to catch her," Tully said. "She's changed. She actually seems to really like me now."

"That's the biggest batch of braggin' I ever did hear. Not that being ol' Fearsome's hero is anything to brag about." R.J. started in on his ham sandwich.

"It's the pure truth. Didn't you see her make me sit by her? And what about that look she gave me after she read her essay?"

"I was too busy trying not to laugh," R.J. said.

"She's been walking up my heels all morning." Tully put his foot on the dustpan and swept broken glass in. "I tell you, it's weird, but maybe it's better than being her punching bag."

"You might as well eat your lunch," R.J. said. "Your sweeping is taking so much time, we'll have to meet everyone on the playground."

"I'm not hungry." Tully thrust his lunch bag at R.J. and swept under the desks.

By the time they got to the sun-baked playground, Ceroy was organizing a game of dodgeball against the gray brick wall. Honey, her hands tucked into her armpits, slouched in a narrow trapezoid of shade against a palm tree, a piece of spear grass in the corner of her mouth.

"We're in," R.J. said to Ceroy. R.J. and Tully took places against the wall by John Ed and Tookie.

Honey strolled over. "I'm in, too," she said.

"No way." Ceroy spun the ball in his hands. "No girls."

"Oh, yeah?" Honey asked, hands on her

hips. "Who's going to stop me?" She grinned a challenge at Ceroy, twirling the spear grass in her mouth. And then she laughed in a way that made Tully's back shiver.

There was an uncomfortable silence while Ceroy looked away, a whiteness around his lips.

"Come on, Honey," Tookie said slowly, cracking his knuckles. "It's the first day of school, and nobody wants any problems. Why don't you get another ball and start your own game?"

"You've got the only ball," Honey said. "So maybe I'll just take this one and start my own game."

Honey grabbed the ball, but Ceroy held on tight. "Let go, Honey!"

Honey tugged hard at the ball. "You're just wasting time, Ceroy."

Ceroy's face colored. "Give it!" he yelled.

Some fifth-grade boys rushed over, hoping to see a fight.

"A crowd's gathering," R.J. said, "and a teacher will be over here any minute."

"Don't buck your luck, Ceroy," John Ed urged. "She'll get you later if you don't let her play."

Ceroy, his face red, let go of the ball and yelled, "Then you're It, Honey."

Honey held the ball in front of her with both hands, rocking from heel to toe in her black patent shoes. Her eyes watched like a stalking cat's while the boys yelled dares and made faces at her and leapt around in front of the wall. John Ed stuck his rear end out boldly, and the ball shot from Honey's hands. It bounced off his backside, and John Ed was It. Honey took his place at the wall.

John Ed couldn't throw straight, and the ball hit the wall six times before Tully felt sorry for him and let himself be hit on the shoulder.

At one end of the wall, Tookie pretended to be tying his shoes, but Tully knew he was watching and would jump out of the way as soon as the ball left Tully's hands. He could always get John Ed, but that was no challenge. He didn't want to encourage Honey by paying attention to her, so that left R.J. and Ceroy, at the other end of the wall. Ceroy hated to be It and almost never was. He was the one Tully wanted. Tully threw a couple of shots at Tookie, missing on purpose. He faked another shot at Tookie, but turned suddenly and hit Ceroy on the hand.

"Come on, Ceroy," everyone singsonged. "You're It."

"He didn't get me," Ceroy yelled. "He almost did, but the ball bounced here." He pointed to a place on the wall.

"Yeah?" R.J. said. "Why's your hand red?"

"Okay," Ceroy shouted. "It's not fair, but I don't want to be a bad sport."

Ceroy was tall and rangy, and he hunched his shoulders as he stood with the ball. He took two quick shots at John Ed and missed him by inches. John Ed was an easy out, and missing him was a blow to Ceroy. His face flushed, and splashes of red blotched his neck. He took a quick shot at Honey's head, but she ducked and the ball ricocheted back to him. He tried for R.J., but R.J. leapt to the side, landing on Tully's foot.

Tully yowled and grabbed for his foot. At the same time, Ceroy shot the ball into his stomach so hard that he folded like a rag doll against the wall.

"Hey, man," R.J. yelled. "He wasn't ready!"

Tully held his stomach and gasped for air. He could hear the bickering and shouting over his head, but he was too busy trying to get his wind back to focus on it. Honey crouched beside him, and he scrambled backward against the wall. Her face was red and sweat-streaked, and her eyes were chilly green.

"Ceroy, you jerk," she screamed, "you done it on purpose." Suddenly, Honey launched herself at Ceroy, her head down like a bull going for a red flag. Ceroy grunted as Honey slammed him to the ground. She sat on his chest, grabbed his hair, and banged his head against the blacktop.

"You're a dirty, rotten cheat," Honey yelled.

The rest of the class had gathered and stood

paralyzed, watching Honey. Tully got to his feet.

"Stop it!" he shouted. "Let him go right now!" Tully pulled Honey's arm hard, and she let go of Ceroy.

"Miss Whistler's coming," Rhoda Webb gasped. She was a bug-eyed thing who almost never talked, so when she did, people listened.

Honey stood up, wet semicircles under her armpits. Her dress stuck to the back of her legs. She stabbed an accusing finger at Ceroy, who was still on the ground. "You don't never hurt Tully, you hear?"

Tully burned with embarrassment. Last year she'd picked on him, and now she was his champion? This same nightmare of a girl? Why wouldn't she just leave him alone? Hadn't he already been through enough?

"I don't need you to help me," he blurted out, his face blazing.

Honey's face flushed as red as her hair, and she looked almost ready to cry.

Tully took Ceroy's arm and pulled him up.

Ceroy was blinking and shaking his head to get the stars out.

As they walked back to class, R.J. said, "Sorry I didn't believe you, Tully. After everything that happened last year, I just couldn't wrap my brain around the idea of ol' Fearsome liking you."

5

Tully avoided looking at Honey for the rest of the afternoon, but when the final bell rang, she pressed a note into his hand. He shot out of the room and ran down the road toward home without talking to anyone. He was almost at the gate to the ranch before he finally opened the note.

I hope you like me.

For the second time that day, he asked himself the same question. Wasn't it better to have Honey like him than to be her victim? A vision of Ceroy's head in the dirt rose up. Tully cringed. But why me? he asked himself. He didn't want to be anything to her. Something had to be done, he knew for certain, but he had no idea what that something might be.

★   ★   ★

That night he sprawled on the barn floor and tried to do his long division homework. The barn was open at both ends, and a breeze from the southeast, crisp with the odor of cord grass and the saltiness of the Gulf, wafted all around him. Moths circled in the light, throwing shadows on his notebook paper. A mouse skittered along the wall, and Spareribs, the barn cat, streaked after it.

He was feeling lonely, when Bigun came in with a small white box and a pen, a sheepish grin on his face.

"Not again! Aren't you gettin' too old for this sort of thing?" Tully teased. "Seems like you were sixty on your last birthday." Bigun couldn't read or write, so every time he had a fight with his girlfriend, Suzy, Tully had to write a mushy letter for him.

Bigun's smile vanished quicker than a rabbit down a hole. "Aren't you a smart bundle of mouth? A man's never too old for love."

"I'll write it, but I'm not figurin' out what to say," Tully said. He took the pen and the grocery store stationery and waited.

"Okay, just write," Bigun said.

When he had finished dictating, Tully read the letter back to him:

Darlin',

I'm sorry that we squabbled like a couple of chickens. I guess I have to admit it was my own fault. I'm not used to having a loving woman. Please forgive me.

Your Kissbug

"Your *Kiss*bug? Sick," Tully said after he finished writing "Suzy" on an envelope. Bigun's letters were so sappy.

He put the envelope next to the letter, then read the letter again to himself. "Does this sort of letter writing really work with girls?"

Bigun drew himself up proudly, pleased with Tully's question. "Oh, yeah. Suzy won't even speak to me now, but after she reads this letter, she'll be happy as a hog in a potato patch." His smile made little laugh wrinkles at the corners of his eyes.

"What if you want to get rid of a girl that's really pestering you?"

"Aw, well, you're probably just better off to tell her outright. But let her down easy, though, if you know what I mean."

Tully fidgeted uncomfortably. Bigun probably thought he was talking about some little slip of a girl who would cry if you looked at her the wrong way. He'd started to talk to Bigun or Red a hundred times the year before when Honey plagued him. He even came close to talking to his mother. They certainly knew something was wrong when he was touchy and had bad dreams again and again. Yet each time he came close to confiding, he was too ashamed to tell them a girl was bothering him.

"But this girl can really be hateful, Bigun. I don't want her to love me, but I don't want her to hate me, either."

"You afraid she might turn on you?" Bigun asked.

Tully felt his face color, and he chewed his lower lip.

"You can try a note, but if that don't work, just ignore her." Bigun cleaned his fingernails with his pocketknife.

Tully's stomach tightened. Could you ignore a herd of stampeding cattle? Still, Bigun had said to try a note, and Tully grabbed onto the hope that it would work.

He thought for a while and wrote:

No offense. You're okay, but I don't like you nor hate you neither. Please don't bother me anymore.

Tully read it over several times. It was polite, he thought, but firm, and he felt good for the first time that day. He took another envelope from the box and wrote "Honey" on it.

Bang! Risky kicked at her stall door and snorted. Tully dropped the stationery and ran to the stall where the mare paced back and forth nervously.

"She's been jittery all day," Bigun said.

"Maybe the foal's coming," Tully said hopefully.

"Maybe. Maybe not."

"I'm going to sit up with her all night and wait," Tully said.

"No you're not," Tully's mother said from the barn door. "Mares are secretive about giving birth. She's already a few days late, and you could delay it even more."

"It's after ten," Bigun said, looking at his watch. "You've got school tomorrow. Go on to bed, Tully."

Tully started to argue, but he realized it wouldn't do any good. He crossed the yard to the house and went up the stairs and through the hallway to his room. Pulling off his boots and dumping his clothes in a heap on the floor, he padded down the hall to the bathroom. Once in bed, he fought sleep so that he could slip back out to Risky's stall after the others had turned in. But the night was so quiet that the surf in the distance sounded like a long-drawn sigh. The sheets smelled so good, he fell asleep in two winks.

He awoke in the first faint gray light of dawn. Thinking a noise had roused him, he lay in bed, listening. The only sound he heard was the windmill as it creaked and turned behind the house.

Tully pulled on his jeans and boots and ran out to the barn. The sky was lightening to the east, and birds made first-light noises. He heard Risky squeal, and he knew this was the sound that had wakened him.

Bigun and Red were down at the end of the barn by Risky's stall. Bigun looked upset. It was so quiet, Tully thought he could hear the dust ticking in the barn.

"What's wrong?" he called from the barn door, his heart pounding wildly at his rib cage.

"Risky's had a filly, but she won't feed it," Red called.

Tully ran down the aisle, hazy with dust, to the stall where a little tar-paper-black filly lay in the corner. Still wet and shivering, her ears plastered down, she lifted her head from the hay and gave a breathy whinny. From what he could see in the iron gloom of the barn, the filly looked wonderful. She had a white blaze on her forehead. She seemed alert as she shook her head, trying to get the fluid out of her nose.

Risky was a few feet away, munching oats at the hay feeder. She looked back briefly along the stretch of her body at the filly, then returned to her oats.

The filly struggled to her feet and wobbled.

She looked perfectly sound, tottering on spindly legs as she approached Risky.

Bigun sighed. "I'm afraid Risky's going to kick the liver and lights out of that poor little foal."

As the foal nuzzled her udder, Risky squealed, pinned back her ears, and lashed out with her foot. She caught the filly in the neck and sent her flying across the stall.

"No!" Tully screamed. He threw open the stall door with shaking hands and put one arm under the filly's neck and the other under her hips. Her silky coat was wet, and she faltered some when he walked her out.

"Bigun," Tully called, "can't we phone the vet in Port Call and get whatever all we need to feed her? Why didn't you take her out the first time it happened?"

"I've never seen a mare that wouldn't come around and nurse eventually. Risky never was dependable in a tight squeeze, though." Bigun's mouth wrinkled in disgust.

Red rubbed the filly's quivering withers with a towel. "No need to be hard-spoken, Bigun. After all, the boy loves Risky."

There was a taste in Tully's mouth like he was going to be sick. He had to swallow hard against the tightness in his throat, and the inside of his face hurt like it was all squeezed together. He stroked the filly's velvety ears.

"I never even thought for a minute something like this could happen," Tully said.

"Don't take it so hard, boy," Red said quietly. There was a white half-moon across Red's brow from the shadow of his hat. "I used to work at a horse-breeding farm. Some mares just don't have a maternal instinct. They're still good using horses, though."

"I don't know if I'll ever be able to ride her again." Tully swallowed hard. "The way I feel right now, I don't even want to see her."

Tully's mother brought his breakfast out to the barn, but he couldn't eat. Bigun brought his books and his backpack with his lunch and a T-shirt for school. Tully didn't want to go to school, but he wanted to get away from Risky.

"I hate to ask you at a time like this." Bigun put his arm around Tully's neck and walked with him to the gate. "Will you take my letter to Suzy at the Island Store on your way to school?" Bigun handed him both envelopes. "I sealed up yours, too."

Tully had forgotten all about the letters. His problems with Honey Kotcher seemed far away.

"I'll take it if you'll do something for me," Tully said. "Move Risky out to the pasture behind the barn. I don't want to see her when I get home."

"You sure?" Bigun asked.

"I'm sure." His voice cracked, and he kicked the flat dried shell of a tree pod with the toe of his boot.

Tully trudged up the road to the village, his hands pocketed and his head cupped between his shoulder blades. He barely noticed the puffs of creamy white blooms atop the yucca plants' tangled leaves, or the smell of Cherokee roses in the air.

The cowbell clanked over the door at the Island Store, and Tully saw Mr. Filbert putting the latest issues of *People* and *Newsweek* magazines on the rack. Suzy was counting the money in her cash register.

"Hey, Tully," Suzy said, glancing up. She

was a small, plain woman, not much older than Tully's mother.

"Hey, Suzy." Tully handed her the envelope. "Here's another note from Bigun."

"That stubborn old sockwad." There was a little bit of a smile on one side of her face. "I ought to tear this up."

Suzy said the same thing every time Tully delivered a note. But after a few hours, she would call, and Bigun would get in his truck and visit her at the boardinghouse.

Suzy called out to him as he was leaving. "Here, Tully." She handed him a bag of malted milk balls. "You look like Old Man Trouble's only son. Maybe this will cheer you up."

"Thanks." Tully half smiled. He could barely remember the days when his troubles had been so small that a bag of candy actually did comfort him.

6

R.J. fell in step with Tully outside the long, two-story school building. To Tully, it seemed to throw a dark shadow. Etched into red sandstone above the main doorway was a legend that read: LOVE KNOWLEDGE, SEEK WISDOM, although maybe it should have said: "Enter at Your Own Risk."

Tully told R.J. about Risky and the foal. Talking about it made everything seem more believable.

"What are you going to do about the foal?" R.J. asked.

Tully shrugged. "Raise her as an orphan." He couldn't help feeling sorry for himself. "I guess the way my life is going, I shouldn't have been surprised that it happened."

"At least you've got a baby horse."

"Filly," Tully corrected.

"Filly," R.J. repeated. "I'd like to have

one of those. All I've got is a dog and a gold-fish."

In class, Tully avoided looking at Honey. While Miss Whistler took attendance, he sat rigidly and tried to decide how to give Honey the note. If he could get her off his back, at least some of his problems would be solved.

That afternoon during math, Tully finished his work sheet quickly. He slipped the envelope with Honey's name on it into his back pocket. Taking his paper to Miss Whistler's desk, where she was busy grading papers, he placed it on top of the others.

Honey still labored over her work sheet. This is it, Tully thought. He lightly pitched the envelope into her lap and took his seat across the aisle from her.

Tully looked at her out of the corner of his eye. What's she doing? Instead of opening the note inside her desk, like anyone else, she made a great show of ripping the envelope open in plain view of everyone.

"Honey Kotcher!" Miss Whistler said. "What are you doing?"

"Reading a note Tully passed me," Honey announced loudly.

Miss Whistler stared at Tully for an eternity, her lips pursed. "Well, stand up, Honey, and read it to all of us."

Honey stood and faced the class, two pink spots blazing on her cheeks. " 'Darlin', I'm sorry that we squabbled like a couple of chickens.' " Honey slowly read the words.

"Wait a minute," Tully blurted. "That's the wrong letter!"

"Tullis!" Miss Whistler stood up. "You're in enough trouble. Now go ahead, Honey."

Honey squinted at the paper. " 'I guess I have to admit it was my own fault. I'm not used to having a loving woman. Please forgive me.' "

Snickers erupted from different parts of the room, until the whole class was laughing.

Honey giggled and looked sideways at him.

"And it's signed, 'Your Kissbug,' " Honey added.

"Your *what?*" Miss Whistler shouted over the racket.

Tully shook his head in his hands. He wanted to die. His life was one big rotten disaster after another.

"Your *Kissbug,*" Honey squealed between giggles.

There was so much laughter in the room that Miss Whistler clapped her speckled hands. When that didn't work, she shuffled to the light switch and turned it on and off, screeching, "Hush!" until the room was quiet.

"That's Bigun's note, Miss Whistler," Tully shouted so that she'd hear him.

"Whose? Oh, let me see that." Miss Whistler took the note from Honey. Her lips compressed tightly while she read it.

"Looks like your handwriting to me, Tullis Webster."

Here and there a giggle rippled across the room. Tully recognized Ceroy's high-pitched cackle.

"Yes, but Honey got Suzy's note, so Suzy must have gotten Honey's, and . . . "

Miss Whistler sighed, and glared at him with hard brown eyes. "Well, Romeo, I can see that I'm going to have to separate you from your

Juliet, or one of them, anyway. At least *Suzy* isn't in my class. Tullis, you stay there, where I can keep an eye on you. Honey, change desks with Ceroy Taylor."

Tully sank lower in his seat, a faint buzzing in his ears.

"Who's Suzy?" Honey kept asking nobody in particular as she cleared out her desk.

Tully spent the rest of the afternoon in a daze of humiliation. He had to stay after school and write "I will not pass notes" one hundred times. He was glad that he didn't have to face anyone, but he felt more hopeless by the second.

When Tully was finished, he dragged his feet through the dark-green halls to the front door of the school. He passed Dane Dugan, mopping the scuffed wood floors. Dane looked as depressed as Tully felt.

"What are you doing here so late?" Tully asked.

"What does it look like? I'm mopping the floor."

"Why?" asked Tully.

"I haven't got the thirty-five dollars to pay

for the window I broke, so Mr. Barnes is making me work it off after school." Dane pushed the wet mop around. "One lousy dollar a day is all the old booger's paying me."

"That's rotten," Tully said.

"You think that's rotten?" Dane leaned against the mop handle. "Listen to this. I'm missing more than a month of football practice. I won't even get to play in the first game."

"Oh, man, that really stinks."

Tully shook his head and walked out of the building into the windy sunshine. Life was too unfair. Dane Dugan made one bad pitch, and they turned him into a janitor. Tully tried to keep Honey out of trouble, and it had already caused no end of misery for him.

Ceroy and Tookie were shooting baskets against the backboard in the schoolyard. Tully tried to make himself small as he hurried by along the gravel road.

"Hey, *Kissbug,*" Tookie yelled. "Congratulations on your new girlfriend."

"She's not my girlfriend," Tully yelled back.

"You could've fooled me." Ceroy sauntered into the road in front of him. "It was your handwriting on the note. Miss Whistler said."

"Yeah, but the note was meant for someone else." Tully's face was burning hot. He tried to walk around Ceroy, but Ceroy stepped in front of him again.

"First you let her fight your battles, then you write her mushy notes," Ceroy said. "You're turning into quite a lover boy."

Tully jabbed his elbow at Ceroy to get away from him, but Ceroy pushed his way in front of him again. Then Ceroy laughed and clapped his hands once.

"Yessir. From Boo Hoo to Kissbug." Ceroy laughed. "Now ain't that a shame?"

Tully dropped his books, and his fist shot out and smacked Ceroy hard on the knob of his nose.

"Oooah," Ceroy grunted, cupping his hand over his nose. When he pulled his hand away, there was blood on it. The look on Ceroy's face changed from surprise to injured rage. He grabbed the front of Tully's shirt while Tully grabbed the front of his. They stood glaring, each waiting for the other to let go and throw another punch.

From the corner of his eyes Tully saw Tookie, his hands on his hips. But too late he realized he shouldn't have let his attention wander. Ceroy broke the clinch and drove a fist into Tully's stomach. The air went out of Tully with a great *Whuff!* so that he had to ward off Ceroy's blows while he caught his breath. He took punches on his arms, chest, and shoulders until he finally moved in and threw one to the side of Ceroy's head.

Ceroy shook his head before they pitched into each other again. Suddenly, they were in a clinch again, which Tully didn't want to break for fear he'd be too vunerable.

"Hey," someone yelled across the yard. "What's going on over there?"

Mr. Frazer, the janitor, came out the back door with a pile of erasers.

"Here comes Frazer," Tookie shouted, and pulled Ceroy's arm. "If he catches us fighting, we'll be pounding erasers for him."

"I'll get you for this, Tully," Ceroy snarled. He and Tookie dashed across the schoolyard.

Still raw and angry, Tully got up and brushed the gravel from his skinned palms. He snatched up his books and headed down the road.

"Hey, boy!" Mr. Frazer called after him. "Are you all right?"

"Yeah, I'm just great," Tully lied. He walked home with his head down. He hated Honey, pure and simple. She'd ruined his life, and now he was fighting with Ceroy. He'd never had a real fight with anyone.

At the ranch, Tully went right to the barn, where he found Red with the little filly in Risky's old stall. Red had cleaned her up and brushed her until her coat was so smooth that it shone like silk. She was dark as a pile of black cats, except for the blaze on her forehead.

"I taught her to drink," Red said, beaming. "Looky here." He stuck his forefinger into a pail of milk and held it up to the filly's mouth. She sucked on it and then lapped milk from the pail.

"Why don't you go on up to the house and rest," Tully said. "I'll sit with her a spell."

Red slapped his knees and stood up. He put a hand, rough as sandpaper, on Tully's neck. "Don't grieve so, boy. I can't hardly stand seeing you let down like this. It's all going to work out."

"I just keep thinking about all the mares I've seen nickering and fussing over their foals. What's wrong with Risky?"

"She's an opinionated horse, all right," Red said in his gravelly voice. "She spends a lot of time trying to make things happen the way she figures they should."

"Do you think she could learn to be a mother?"

Red shook his head. "No, Tully, I'm afraid you're the only animal she's got time for, and this here little filly just ain't in her plans."

"I wanted it to be different, that's all." He was as mad at Risky as he was at Honey Kotcher. Tully was afraid an orphaned horse would never grow up to be quite normal.

"Well," Red said, walking out of the barn, "if God was to listen to the prayers of buzzards, there'd be dead cows all over the dunes. Maybe it'll all work out for the best. By the way." Red looked shy all of a sudden. "I named her Valentine, seeing as how she's so sweet and all. You can change it if you want."

"No," Tully said. "I like it. We can call her Val for short."

The foal had settled on the hay for a nap. Tully lay down beside her and put his head in her mane, his anger still smarting.

"It's been an awful day for both of us," Tully whispered. He closed his eyes. The filly's breathing was steady and even. "Things can't get much worse. Maybe that means they're going to get better."

Valentine might not be Risky's choice, but she was theirs now. His plan to shake Honey Kotcher may have backfired, but he was sure to come up with a new plan. The next one would work. It had to.

7

It was almost dark outside when Tully left the barn. In the side yard, he washed at the garden faucet amid the mission figs and the sunflowers and he wiped the dust from his boots. The house was lit up as if it held a pile of embers, every window throwing rectangles onto the lawn. When he entered the kitchen, the smells of dinner reminded him how hungry he was.

His mother sat at the kitchen table, reading the *Port Call Express*. She hated to cook just as much as she loved to keep the books for the ranch. She and Bigun had worked out an arrangement when Tully's father died and Bigun came to the ranch as foreman. When bills needed to be paid, supplies ordered, extra hands hired, or money borrowed from the bank, Tully's mother was the one who did it, working from her little office behind the kitchen. With Red's help, Bigun did most everything else.

The one thing Bigun never wanted help with was the cooking. A fan whirred loudly above the stove, where Bigun was making a batch of beef stew while Red watched. Bigun's arms were sprinkled with flour from the biscuits. When Bigun turned his back, Red lifted the pot lid and Tully dipped a ladle in for a taste.

Bigun wheeled around and smacked Red and Tully on their heads with a wooden spoon.

"We're starving," Tully said.

"Let them have a bite, Bigun," Tully's mother said. "What's got into you?"

"I get tired of people snoopin' around my kitchen, sniffin' and tastin' all the ingredients in my cookery."

Red got a can from the pantry and opened it with the electric can opener.

"What are you doin' now?" Bigun shouted. "You'll ruin your appetite."

"I'm goin' to eat these here Vienna sausages." Red grinned at Tully and chomped on a sausage. "Now, a Vienna sausage is a smart food, seeing as how it knows where it's from. Like a Brussels sprout. Bigun's stew is a confused food."

Tully and his mother laughed. Tully knew Red was trying to cheer him up.

Bigun looked through the kitchen window, then suddenly grabbed a rifle by the door and rushed out to the yard, followed by Tully and Red. They watched as Bigun aimed his rifle at a spot under the live oak tree. It made a *ca-rack!* that caused doves to fly out of the tree. Bark and sand and leaves scattered in every direction. Spareribs, the cat, streaked away from the bushes and ran to the barn.

"I am going to shoot Spareribs if he don't quit stalkin' the doves and their babies in that oak tree," Bigun said.

Back in the kitchen, Bigun slammed the screen door behind him. "I like dove calls," he added.

"Tomcats stalk birds," Tully said. "At least some animals around here are doing what comes natural."

Bigun put the food on the table. There it was, one of Tully's favorite dinners: beef stew with big chunks of potatoes, homemade biscuits, and in the middle of the table a bowl of salad with Bigun's own dressing. As Tully pressed his fork into the meat, so tender he didn't have to cut it, he looked at Bigun gratefully. But Bigun just pushed his food around with the prongs of his fork and glared at them.

"I can't believe my eyes," Bigun fussed. "Y'all eat like a bunch of monkeys with bad table manners."

Mrs. Webster put her spoon down. "You're carrying on like an old granny tonight. Did you work out in the sun without your hat on?"

Tully looked at Bigun. It dawned on him for the first time what was wrong. He'd been so worried about his own problems that he hadn't thought about anyone else.

After dinner, Tully quickly cleared the table. While his mother and Red washed the dishes, he followed Bigun out to the front porch. Tully sat down on the steps and listened to the night hawks *peent* and the lowing of cattle far off in the dunes.

Bigun leaned back in a rickety chair, his hands curled over the ends of the arms. He was frowning like an old toad.

"Did Suzy call you?" Tully asked.

"No," Bigun grumbled. "I finally called her and she hung up on me three different times."

"Bigun," Tully said. "You accidentally switched those letters. Honey Kotcher, that girl I told you about? She got the sappy one meant for Suzy. That means Suzy got the one I wrote, telling Honey to leave me alone. My guess is that Suzy's hopping mad right now."

"My lord." Bigun let the front legs of his chair come down hard on the porch. "I thought for certain sure she'd decided to throw me over."

Bigun got out of the chair and headed for his truck. "I've got to get to the boardinghouse quick. I have some explainin' to do."

On Wednesday, Tully's class had art in the cafeteria. They pushed two long cafeteria tables together and sat side by side in metal chairs. Matagorda School couldn't afford different teachers for music and art, so Mr. Hubert, a squat, gray-haired man with glasses, was both. Today he came around with a cart piled high with paper-towel tubes, Styrofoam, pipe cleaners, and construction paper.

"We're making collages today. Express yourselves!" Mr. Hubert bellowed as the kids grabbed poster board and other materials. "I'll hang these in the hallways when you're finished. And remember, class, artists always title their work."

Tully tried to make a corral with the tubes and pipe cleaners. He was only half finished and hadn't even put the cows in the corral when Mr. Hubert began to hold finished posters up for the class to see.

Rhoda Webb had named her collage "Shrimp Boat," and it actually resembled one if you turned your head to the side. Ceroy had named his "Bombs Exploding"—he'd cut Styrofoam in the shape of mushroom clouds and painted them gray.

"Ah, Honey," Mr. Hubert said, staring at her poster, his head tilted. "Stand up and tell us about your work."

The center of Honey's masterpiece was a giant red Styrofoam heart with pink spots on it.

It had lots of pipe-cleaner legs coming out of the sides and feelers made of black yarn. Tully didn't like the look of this. He chewed his bottom lip, and his armpits felt sweaty.

"Oh, no," R.J. said out of the corner of his mouth.

"This is an excellent use of materials, Honey, and it's colorful," Mr. Hubert said, obviously impressed.

Teachers always seemed to like Honey's artwork, but did Mr. Hubert have to go on and on? Ceroy and Tookie looked at Tully and grinned.

"What's the title of your collage, Honey?" Mr. Hubert finally asked.

"Can anyone guess?" Honey swished her skirt as she peeled Elmer's glue from her fingers.

" 'Kissbug,' " John Ed called out.

Honey beamed.

"Yeah! It's a kissbug," Carrie Ellis called.

"It's really Tully, though," Ceroy said, loud enough for everyone to hear, as he nudged Tookie in the ribs. With that, giggles broke out.

Honey looked at Tully as though the very air he breathed were made of cookies and cake.

"That's enough now." Mr. Hubert quickly turned to Tookie's art.

Tully put his head down on the table. His cheeks burned, and he could feel a trickle of sweat between his shoulder blades. He continued gluing pipe cleaners all over his poster board, but the corral didn't matter to him anymore.

"Honey Kotcher's love is as fearsome as her hate," R.J. whispered.

R.J. was absent on Thursday, and Tully felt alone all morning. He kept to himself, finishing all his work and even cleaning out his desk.

"Tullis," Miss Whistler called. "Please take this note to the principal's office." She looked at her watch. "It's almost time for lunch, so you can meet us in the cafeteria when you're finished."

Tully took the note and his brown lunch bag from his desk. On his way out the door, Ceroy slapped him on the back and simpered, "How's the kissbug today?"

Tully's face burned in embarrassment as he walked down the hall. When he passed the bathroom, a small boy came out.

"Hey, Kissbug?" he called after Tully. "I don't want to kiss you."

"Great," Tully muttered. "Even the second graders know."

In the cafeteria, kids Tully didn't even know snickered as he walked by. It was as if he were in one of those dreams where he looked down and discovered he'd come to school in his underwear. Honey was sitting with Miss Whistler. Tully would have sat with John Ed, but John Ed laughed so hard when he approached the table that milk ran out of his nose. The only spot left was a place by the new girl, Nell Bailey. She and Rhoda Webb sat at a table by themselves, reading.

Tully made a great to-do about taking the food out of his brown bag so he wouldn't seem rattled by the laughter, but he could barely eat. He took a bite of his roast beef sandwich and chewed. He tried to swallow, but the meat had swollen in his mouth, and he had to go on chewing. There wasn't enough air in the cafeteria. With all his might, Tully wished he never had to show his face in school again.

Something was jerked from his back. He swiveled around to see Miss Whistler holding a drawing of a heart-shaped red bug with spots. Underneath, someone had written:

I'M A KISSBUG. KISS ME QUICK!

"Is there nothing you won't do for attention, Tullis Webster?"

Tully tried to swallow again, but his mouth was dry and the meat just wouldn't go down. "I didn't do it. Someone must have taped it on when my back was turned." Tully remembered Ceroy's hearty slap on the back.

Miss Whistler stared at Tully without saying anything.

"Don't speak with your mouth full," she said before she huffed off.

"Do you really like that girl?" Nell asked.

"I hate her." Tully finally swallowed the meat, his eyes slanting like a toad's with the effort. "I didn't write that note to her, either. It was all a mistake."

Rhoda looked at Nell and whispered, "When we were in the fourth grade, Honey got mad because I wouldn't let her cheat off me. She drew dirty pictures on the bathroom wall and made Sissy West tell the teacher that I did it."

"Did you get in trouble?" Nell asked.

"I had to scrub the bathroom walls and eat lunch in the principal's office for a week. Mr. Barnes probably still thinks I'm a pervert." Rhoda blinked and swallowed.

The idea that anyone would think Rhoda was a pervert made Tully smile.

"Doesn't anyone ever tell on her?" Nell asked.

"She'd probably hurt you," Rhoda said, "and if she didn't, she'd find some sneaky way to get back at you without getting caught. It's usually not worth it."

"Why does she act that way?" Nell asked.

"My momma says it's because her daddy's mean, and those bruises she gets on her arms sometimes are because he hits her."

Nell's blue eyes popped wide open. "He hits her?"

Tully felt a rush of pity as he remembered

the ugly bruise on Honey's arm that day at the wharf.

"That's right," Rhoda said. "I think the teachers know it. She can be sneaky so she doesn't get caught, but they still let her get away with so much." Rhoda leaned across the table and lowered her voice. "The Kotchers' next-door neighbors told my momma they saw him punch her once and they hear him yelling at her a lot. Sometimes they hear her cry."

"Where's her mother?" Nell asked.

Rhoda shrugged her shoulders. "Who knows? Momma says she's been gone since Honey was no more than four or five. Never even comes back for a visit."

"If he hits her, how come someone doesn't report him?" Nell asked.

"What good would it do?" Rhoda scratched her arm. "She doesn't have any other relatives on the island. Who else but kin would take Honey Kotcher in?"

A couple of years ago, Honey's father had delivered fish to the ranch. He was a big hulking fisherman with arms the size of a side of beef and a neck like an ox. Even though Tully's own father was dead, he had his mother, and Bigun and Red were like family. No one had ever laid a hand on him.

What would it be like to be Honey?

8

On Friday, someone put a horse turd in Miss Whistler's desk before school started. When Miss Whistler found it, she sucked in her breath with such force that the papers stirred on her desk. No one saw who had done it, but Tully knew she suspected him, because she tapped her pencil against the edge of her desk and shot a sour look at him.

Honey's bright-green eyes tracked him silently wherever he went. She sent him a silly little note that said:

> Dear Tully,
> Guess who?
> Your Kissbug

Tully ripped the note into tiny pieces and threw it into the wastebasket. He'd rather receive a horse turd than a note from Honey.

Even when Honey wasn't around, he felt her lurking like an alligator, swinging her tail back and forth. That afternoon, Tully heard smacking noises behind his back in the hall. His eyes were constantly on guard, in case someone tried to slip another kissbug on his back.

Last year the class had felt sorry for him when Honey called him Boo Hoo, and the nickname never caught on with anyone but Honey. After all, almost everyone was Honey's victim at one time or another. But this was different; it was only the end of the first week of school, and Tully felt sure he'd be known as "Kissbug" permanently if he didn't do something soon.

Miss Whistler made him stay after school to do over his math work sheet; it had so many mistakes that he'd made holes in the paper erasing them. R.J. waited for him outside the door.

"Ol' Fearsome's really got you shook up, don't she?" R.J. asked when he came out.

Tully nodded. "It was better when she hated me."

"Naw." R.J. let the air whistle through his

teeth. "She's even bigger now than she was last year. It could be dangerous."

"True," Tully said. He recalled how last year on the playground Honey had suddenly, without provocation, slapped him so hard on the top of his head that he saw stars shining between the blue veins in his eyeballs. It had happened so swiftly few of his classmates noticed. Red-faced, Honey had said loudly, for the benefit of the playground monitor, "Wasps! Trying to sting poor Tully!"

Tully and R.J. stopped in the hall to watch Dane, perched at the top of a ladder, washing windows. He looked miserable wiping the soapsuds off the panes, as he gazed out the window to where the football team practiced their tackles on the playing field.

"Poor ol' Dane." R.J. smiled.

"At least he doesn't have Honey Kotcher in love with him," Tully said.

"Too bad. It would serve him right." R.J. jabbered on, but Tully wasn't listening.

What if Dane *did* have Honey in love with him? Tully wondered.

"If Honey thought she could have Dane Dugan for a boyfriend, she'd never give a shrimp like me another thought, would she?" Tully asked.

"Don't be stupid," R.J. said. "Dane can have any girl he wants. What would he want with Honey?"

"It's just a thought," Tully said.

"Let's get out of here," R.J. said. "Maybe we'll have time to go to your place and see the filly."

Tully needed time to think. He'd been thinking hard since his plan backfired on Tuesday, and he hadn't come up with a new one. Until now.

"Maybe tomorrow," Tully said. "I think I'll stick around here and help Dane."

"Help Dane?" R.J. asked. "I think Honey Kotcher's made your brain go soft and squishy."

"I'll see you in the morning," Tully called to R.J.'s back.

Tully leaned his forehead against the hall window and snuffed in the comforting smell of chalk dust and floor polish. Against his skin, the window felt surprisingly cool for a September afternoon. As his new plan took shape, Tully's heart did a little hitch.

Dane climbed down the ladder with a bucket of soapsuds. Water sloshed over the sides and splattered the floor. Tully grabbed a mop from the janitor's cart and cleaned it up.

"Thanks." Dane sighed. "Hey, weren't you hanging around after school a few days ago? Do you just like it here, or does the teacher have it in for you?"

"Miss Whistler's on my case pretty good," Tully said, and shook his head.

"That flap-tongued ol' prune hated me, too."

Tully knew that ordinarily Dane wouldn't spend thirty seconds talking to a sixth grader. Misery really does love company, he thought.

"How much do you have left to pay on that window you broke?" Tully asked.

"Thirty dollars after today." Dane moved the ladder down the hall to the next set of windows.

Tully bit his lip. He'd worked cattle in the hot sun all summer for money to buy a ticket and souvenirs when the fair came to Port Call next month. Thirty dollars would set him back. Still . . .

"Maybe I can help you," Tully said. He took a deep breath, like a diver about to plunge into water, then told Dane that there was a girl in his class who liked him, but he didn't like her back.

"The deal is, Dane, I'll pay you thirty dollars to get rid of this girl for me," Tully said.

Dane looked suspicious. "How would I do that?"

Tully shrugged. "Pretend you like her. Ask her to be your girlfriend. She'd forget all about me in a second, and you could get back to football practice."

"She must be a real pain if you're willing to pay me thirty dollars to take her off your hands. What's her name?"

Tully tried to look nonchalant, but his voice cracked. "Honey Kotcher."

"That big ol' girl with the banjo butt?"

"Uh-huh."

"The one that's tough as a tom turkey?"

"She's not so tough," Tully said. "Her heart's as big as the rest of her." A part of

Tully didn't feel good about trying to push Honey off on Dane. But he didn't feel exactly bad, either. Dane looked like he could handle anything.

"No way." Dane started to climb back up the ladder. "I've got my reputation to think about."

"I was just thinking about the team," Tully added, looking out the window. The Matagorda Mustangs were in a huddle now. "Port Call will probably stomp Matagorda, without you in the game. But if you can't, you can't."

Tully started down the hall, his legs as heavy as stone.

"Wait—come back," Dane called. Then he said quietly, "Would anyone have to know about me and this Honey Kotcher?"

Tully thought about it. "I don't care who knows, as long as you get her off my back."

Dane looked around and whispered hoarsely, "Do you think she'd go for a *secret* romance?"

Tully didn't think there was anything at all secretive about Honey. Still, he was sure she'd want Dane any way she could get him.

"Probably," Tully said finally.

"Aw, that's no good." Dane threw up his palms. "There's no place on this island to even spit in secret."

"Coffin Creek," Tully said quickly.

Coffin Creek was a seep spring within spitting distance of the old pioneer graveyard on the island. There were stories that a cattle thief named Rider McCall came out of his grave nightly to roam up and down the creek bed, never stopping to rest. A hundred years earlier, the ranchers, tired of his thieving ways, had cut off his ears and thrown them into the creek. Folks walking by the graveyard at night claimed to see the light from his fire pan swinging in the darkness as he searched for his ears.

"Are you kidding?" Dane asked. "Coffin Creek is haunted."

"That's why it's perfect," Tully said. "Hardly anybody goes there."

Dane's eyes were as round as a hoot owl's.

"What's the matter?" Tully narrowed his eyes.

"Well, I'm not scared of Coffin Creek," Dane said, "but she would be."

How to put it? Tully thought. "Honey Kotcher ain't scared of nothin', Dane. I'll give you fifteen dollars on Monday after you ask her to meet you, and the rest later if it works. Now, will you do it or not?"

Dane watched the Matagorda Mustangs run wind sprints in the dusty twilight. "It's the craziest scheme I've ever been involved in, but I'm desperate. I'll meet her after I get through here on Monday. I want to get it over with."

"Yeah," Tully agreed. "If you've got a frog to swallow, don't look at it any longer than you have to. And, Dane, don't try to stiff me, because I'll be there. You won't see me, but I'll be able to see you and hear everything you say."

"There ain't no place to hide along Coffin Creek."

Tully walked down the hall and corkscrewed his head around. "Oh, yeah," Tully said. "There's a place to hide, all right."

A shaft of sunlight struck Dane's face. He

had a strong jaw and a dark shadow over his lip. Anyone could see that he needed to shave. Honey wouldn't be able to resist Dane, and Tully's troubles would finally be over. He felt like running down the hall and screaming with joy.

9

On Saturday morning, Tully jumped into clean Levi's and had breakfast at daybreak. He was too excited about his plans for Dane and Honey to sleep. It seemed a long time till Monday. There was nothing for it but to keep busy.

Out in the barn, the morning air was cool and heavy with the smells of horse manure and scrub cedar. Valentine was lapping milk, and Red was cleaning out the horse stalls. Tully climbed into the loft and kicked down a few dusty bales of hay to scatter for the horses.

Outside the high loft door, mist rose from the ground in the pasture behind the barn. Risky grazed on salt grass near a small herd of cows. She'd already lost most of the weight she'd gained from carrying Valentine.

After Risky finished grazing, she put her nose up and stared at the cows. When she trotted over to them, they ran in a group toward the far side of the pasture. She circled around and brought them back a little, then cut two of the cows away from the others and put them in a corner. The other cows tried to get to them, but Risky stood between them and wouldn't let them by.

Red came up the loft stairs. "It's awful quiet up here."

"Watch this, Red," Tully said.

The cows stood with their heads in the air, bellowing and watching Risky. From time to time, she pretended to graze, and the two separated cows would try to slip by to get with the others. Instantly, Risky would spin around and light after them, sending them back into the corner.

Tully laughed, and then he felt such an overflow of love for Risky that it almost squeezed the wind out of his chest.

"Risky's one of them cutting horses that's so good she'd likely come on an anthill and start cutting the red ants away from the black." Red grinned. "I bet she gives them ol' cows a run for their money all day long."

Tully shook his head. "You know, I hated

Risky when she wouldn't mother Valentine, but I just don't think I can go on hating her."

"Well, hate ain't got a good future, anyways," Red said. He looked at Tully. "I've been riding her some to get her back in shape for you. It's going to be a pretty morning for a ride. If I was you, I'd take off with her before Bigun or your mother finds some chores for you to do," Red said.

In the tack room, Tully took Risky's bridle from a nail. A cottony ball of spider eggs was stuck to the underside of one of the reins, reminding him of how long it had been since he'd ridden her. He pulled his saddle down from the rack and slung it over his shoulder by the horn and reached for the blanket he always used. Spareribs, who lay basking in the sunlight at the entrance to the barn, regarded him with sleepy eyes when he slung the saddle down.

Tully went to the grain bin and scooped yellow oats into a bucket, then walked through the salt grass to the fence and climbed over. Risky had forgotten the cattle and was grazing in the early-morning sunshine. When Tully was close enough, he shook the oat bucket at her. She trotted over to him and pushed her long, sleek nose against his chest. He rubbed her neck before he set the bucket down and let her nose it. While her head was down, he slipped the reins over her neck and bridled her.

He led her to the barn entrance, lifted the blanket, and placed it on Risky's back. He raised the saddle, with the cinch straps draped over the top and one stirrup hung over the horn, and set it on Risky. She snorted, but didn't move. Tully reached under her belly and pulled up the strap and cinched it again and again, then he lifted the stirrup from the saddle horn and let it drop.

He led her through the stone gate to the road. The beach was over a mile away, down the road away from the village. Tully pulled the cinch strap, buckled it, and passed the reins over Risky's head. She stamped and blew impatiently. He put his foot in the stirrup, swung on up, and settled into the saddle. He urged Risky into an easy lope.

Early-morning sunlight poured over them

and made Risky's sorrel coat gleam like liquid fire. At the road's end, they took a cattle trail across the dunes. Risky's hooves raised a wall of sand that covered everything behind them. Even the baked cow plops and deer droppings scattered across the dunes were a powdery white. A skinny coyote bolted across the trail and slithered under a fence. Risky perked up her ears and shied.

By the time they reached the ocean, the sun was a yellow ball over the glass-green water. Tully raised his head and caught the heavy smell of fish and seaweed rolling in on the sea winds. The beach was crowded with gulls and cormorants diving for fish in the rush and re- turn of the foaming waves.

At the water's edge, Tully kicked Risky into a dead run until her ears were back in the wind and her neck and body were stretched out low to the ground. Stunned, a flock of gulls rose screeching and fighting over the water, scatter- ing the haze. Risky's head turned from side to side, and her hooves pounded the wet sand, while spray flew up in Tully's face. A shriek of joy escaped his throat, and when he leaned forward, Risky's legs and the water were a blur beneath him.

It had been months since Risky could run this fast. Tully had almost forgotten the thrill of leaning low along her neck, constantly urging her on until they were both one runner. They rode clear to the upper end of the beach through the morning ground mist.

Tully turned Risky away from the beach, and she plundered up a dune, startling the grazing cattle. Greenhead horseflies swarmed from the salt grass, and flocks of birds flew up and turned to gold in the rising sun.

Tully brought her to a walk. It was good now to wind slowly through the dunes and enjoy the sight of the ranch in the far distance, the palm trees glowing in the light. And good, too, to lean back in the saddle and stretch his legs against the stirrups and feel Risky under him, sweat-soaked and nervous. She began to prance along the road, slinging her head in a froth from side to side.

"Whatever made me think I could stay off a beautiful, ornery thing like you?" He leaned forward and rubbed Risky's neck. Her ears went back, and Tully laughed.

He led Risky to the hitching rail by the barn and took the saddle off her back. She rubbed her rump against the rail and sucked water from the trough.

Valentine ran around the little pen by the barn, kicking. She whinnied and pretended to bite at a fly, then took off running with her head and tail up, making circles.

Tully climbed between the wires of the pen and dropped to the ground like an ape, mimicking Val. She swung her neck at him as if he were a colt. He collapsed in front of her while she nuzzled his shirt and blew on his face.

"Hey!" he yelled, and jumped up as if a fire alarm had sounded. Val leapt and pranced away, while Tully chased her across the pen. Cantering in circles, she finally stopped in front of his mom.

"I'm glad to see you smile for a change, Tully," his mother said. "You've had a hang-dog look about you since school started."

Tully draped an arm over the filly's neck. "I guess I've had a lot on my mind."

Her dark hair was tied back, and her cheeks were flushed. "I see you and Risky made up."

"Yes, ma'am." Tully took a deep breath. "Mama, do you think Risky remembers having a filly?"

"Probably not," Mrs. Webster said.

"Well, then, how about Val? Do you think she knows that Risky cheated her out of having a mother?"

Mrs. Webster brushed hair from Tully's forehead. "She can't miss what she never had. Besides, you and Red take good care of her."

"So no real harm's been done?" Tully asked.

"Well, she takes a lot more time than she would have, had Risky done her job. But other than that, no real harm. We'd be weaning her from Risky in a few months, anyway."

Tully felt as lighthearted as foam hitting the beach. The burden of his anger for Risky had gone, and he'd never realized how heavy it had been until it was lifted.

10

Tully was relieved when Monday finally came. The day started out as promising as the weekend had been. Tully caught sight of Honey talking to Dane by a palm tree before school started. He fingered the fifteen dollars he'd taken from the wallet in his sock drawer that morning.

When Tully saw Dane's face in the square of glass in the classroom door, he asked Miss Whistler for permission to go to the bathroom. In the hall, Dane grabbed him and pushed him into a dusty alcove behind the stairs.

"It's a go," Dane said. "She's gonna meet me at Coffin Creek when I get through here at five o'clock. She wanted to meet me here, but I told her what I had to talk to her about was a big secret. I hope this works."

Tully pressed the fifteen dollars into his hand. "Good luck, Dane."

Tully fought all day to restrain his impatience. He kept to himself and didn't pass notes or chew gum or flip spitballs or do anything that would give Miss Whistler an excuse to keep him after school.

After lunch, Honey called, "Hi, Kissbug," across the room.

Tully examined his bitten nails. There was nothing left to chew, so he slid his head down on his desk. Just a few more hours of this, he thought, and then it will be Dane's problem. He was sure of it.

When the last bell rang, Tully grabbed his books and rushed out of the room. He hurried away from the village, past the lighthouse where the earth sloped down and the ground was sandy and full of crushed shells. His feet crunched the powdery dust until the trail divided into a V, and he followed the right branch down to the graveyard.

The graveyard was set off from the road by a rusted cast-iron fence of arrowhead pickets with an iron gate. Inside, the gravestones sat weathered and freckled with mold and lichens over the mummy-shaped mounds.

In the corner of the yard where folks said

Rider McCall was buried, there was a sunken grave, no marker at the head or foot. Three summers ago, R.J. had been determined to see Rider's ghost. He convinced Tully to go to the graveyard with him on a night when the stars hung so close they could almost scratch the dirt of the dead man's grave. R.J. thought they could buy Rider out, so they buried a mayonnaise jar full of pennies and nickels beside the grave. Tully even stuffed some Monopoly money in at the last minute.

"Bigun told me they buried Rider eight feet deep so's he'd stay put forever," Tully had said that night.

"Shoot," R.J. scoffed. "That just means he's a little closer to Hell than everybody else. They say when he comes out, you can even *smell* Hell."

At that, Tully had lit out for home, but they'd left the money buried all this time.

Tully bent over the grave now and examined the place beside it with the toe of his boot, but the grass, fine as hair, had grown over it.

The cemetery narrowed just above the mouth of a draw where a thready little creek billowed out of the ground and shimmered in the heat and light. Tully jumped down to the pebble shore and surprised a white crane, which rose from the creek, flapping hard into the air. Water spiders skittered across the surface of the creek, as clear and clean as a sheet of glass.

Tully stopped at a crazy wind-shaped oak tree with branches like outthrust witches' fingers, gnarled and frozen, reaching for the sky. Surging waters had washed the earth out from under part of its roots, leaving a cave beneath the tree just large enough for him. Tully crawled in and pulled a curtain of dangling roots in front of him. He drew his legs up tight against his chest and settled down to wait.

He was remembering the afternoon he and R.J. had discovered the root cave, when he heard the graveyard gate snick shut and Honey Kotcher came into view. She was whistling, and her head swiveled as she looked around for Dane. At first, the sunlight was behind her, and Tully had trouble seeing her well. After a time, though, she hunkered down at the edge of the creek and skipped pebbles on the water.

Tully took several deep breaths to calm himself.

Honey cast nervous, jerky glances around her. Tully could tell she didn't like being there alone. He felt the tickle of something crawling across his arm. A large gray spider with long legs dropped from his arm to the ground. Tully sucked his breath in sharply. Above his head, a mass of spiders quivered in the dusty darkness of the tree. He pressed his hands over his mouth so that he wouldn't scream. He sat rigid, his hands cold and wet as a frog. The spiders were trembling in a mass the size of a grapefruit.

"Hey, Dane." Tully heard Honey's voice as the seventh grader jumped down to the shore from the bank above and strolled toward her. "So why did you want to meet me here?" Honey's curly red hair stood out like a fright wig in the wind.

"Did you tell anyone I asked you to meet me?" Dane asked anxiously. Their shadows touched on the ground.

"Naw," Honey said. "You told me not to. What's the big secret, anyways?"

Dane swallowed hard. "I was wondering. Maybe you'd like to be my secret girlfriend."

Honey reared back and put her hands on her hips. "Your what?"

"My secret girlfriend," Dane said quickly. "You know, nobody would know about it but you and me, and maybe we could meet out here now and then."

A gull cried, and Dane glanced around. The shadows were beginning to lengthen.

"I ain't much of a secret girl my ownself," Honey finally said. "Why would it have to be a secret?"

"Oh, you know," Dane said lamely. "It's more romantic that way."

Honey's eyes narrowed. "I've already got a boyfriend, and it ain't no secret."

"How do you know that pipsqueak Webster even likes you?" Dane dug his boot heel into the dirt.

"He wrote me a note, telling me so."

"Well, I asked you to meet me," Dane said. "That's a lot better than a note."

"What would we do when we meet?"

"I don't know," Dane said. "Do you like to fish?"

"Lord, no," Honey said. "I have to clean enough fish for my Pa."

"What do you like to do, then?"

Honey thought for a moment. "Arm wrestle!"

"Arm wrestle?" Dane asked. "What kind of a thing is that to do with a girl?"

Honey swished her hips. "It's fun. I can beat anybody."

"You can't beat me!" Dane said, folding his arms so that his biceps swelled beneath his balled fists. "I'm the strongest guy in the seventh grade."

"I can even beat my daddy arm wrestling." Honey shrugged and walked to a cemetery vault above the ground. Dane followed her.

Tully turned a little so that he could see. Another jumbo spider dropped on his chest and scuttled away. Tully was conscious of a stiffening of the hair at the base of his neck and a shiver along his spine, a sort of bugle call to action in his blood. He took a deep breath and willed himself to sit still.

Honey planted her right elbow on top of the slab and fanned her hand out, her milky freckled fingers sticking up like sausages.

Dane's eyes widened. "Those mitts look like they belong on Sasquatch!"

Honey nodded, her green eyes glittering. "I told you I was good."

Dane placed his elbow on the vault. He clasped Honey's right hand in a thumb-to-thumb grip and grasped the side of the vault with his left hand.

Honey said, "Ready!" then shouted, "Go!" Immediately she puffed out her cheeks like an adder and bulged her green eyes as if she were having some sort of fit. Dane held his arm rock-steady in the starting position, while she pushed against it.

"C'mon, Dane, push!" Honey screeched. "You can do better than this! Push! C'mon!"

Dane squinched up his face, grunted, and strained against her. Splashes of coppery freckles stood out on Honey's face as she grimaced.

Dane heaved his shoulder toward Honey and managed to push her arm back a couple of inches. He put every bit of his strength into his hand, but Honey pushed his shaking forearm back.

"C'mon, Dane, push! Is this the best you've got?" she taunted.

Honey was gaining. A sheen of sweat broke out on her forehead. Dane, a look of injured rage on his face, put his shoulder into the struggle with all his might, but it wasn't good enough.

Suddenly, Dane's grip went limp as Honey slammed his arm flat to the vault. Dane toppled over sideways, with an earsplitting yell.

"What's wrong, Dane?" Honey's breath came in gasps. "You look like someone backed you into a blowtorch."

Dane writhed on the ground. Finally, he stumbled to his feet, cradling his shoulder. He screamed, "You've dislocated my shoulder, you big palooka!" He lurched to the gate and yelled, "You're loco, you know that? You're just as mean and crazy as your old man."

Tears sprang to Honey's eyes. "That's right, run!" she called after him. She ambled down to the creek, knelt beside it, and scooped cold water on her face.

"My old man ain't crazy," she muttered.

Tully watched her in the twilight. She swiped at the tears on her face with the back of her hand. A frog hopped by, and she picked it up and stroked it. It occurred to Tully that maybe Honey wasn't such a bad person, really, just strange and hard to understand. The notion surprised him.

A spider fell on Tully's nose and scrambled down to his mouth. "Ughhhhhh," Tully grunted without thinking.

Honey shot a startled glance directly at the root cave. Tully caught his breath. Dang, he thought. If she finds me here, she'll drag me out and do Lord knows what. He couldn't let that happen.

On impulse, he called in his best Rider McCall ghost voice, "Honnnnnnneeeeeee! Where are my bloody eeeeeeeears?" He thrust his arm through the tangle of roots, fingers clawing the air.

Honey stumbled backward and stared at the root cave, wide-eyed, the skin paling around her blotchy freckles. Just when he was sure that she was going to turn and run screaming from the graveyard, she frowned, pulled the roots away, and peered in at him.

"Tully!" Honey cried. "Is that you?"

Tully clambered out of the root cave on all fours and stayed that way, staring at the tips of Honey's shoes. His hair was wild, and he was wet and muddy.

Tully, he thought. You are down on your hands and knees at Honey Kotcher's feet. What are you going to do now?

"Spiders all over you!" Honey cried and swiped at his back.

Tully sprang to his feet and hopped about, brushing the spiders from his clothes. Honey pursued him, squealing and swatting at him.

"Everytime I get the feeling you don't like me, you do something that shows me you do," Honey finally said.

"What do you mean?"

"First the note, now this." Honey grinned.

"You were jealous I might like Dane Dugan, and you came here to spy."

"I did not!" Tully yelled. He scrambled up the bank and thundered down the gravel road for home.

In the gathering darkness, Honey's voice trailed after him. "You're my hero, Tully Webster."

11

Dane stood squarely in front of Tully in the hall at school the next morning, his face dark and angry. Tully's lip was purple and swollen from a spider bite, Dane's arm was in a sling.

"I could kill you for getting me involved in this, Webster," Dane snarled. "That girl could break an ax handle on her knee and chew the splinters."

"I'm sorry, Dane," Tully said. "I didn't think she'd hurt you."

"Hurt me? She dislocated my receiving shoulder. Now I'll probably miss the whole season instead of just the first game." He poked Tully in the chest with a finger from his good hand. "And it's your fault." Dane stalked off.

Tully felt a lump growing in his throat. Dane hated his guts, he'd lost fifteen dollars, and Honey liked him more than ever. All he'd gained from this latest scheme was a spider bite. Why didn't he just walk up to Honey and tell her he couldn't stand her? So what if she terrorized him again? How bad could it be?

Tully took his seat, put his books in his desk, and looked around. Ceroy and Tookie were passing a sports magazine to John Ed. Sissy and Carrie whispered at the pencil sharpener, and Rhoda was helping Nell with her homework. They were like pieces of a jigsaw puzzle that had found their places and already fit in. If it weren't for Honey Kotcher, he'd be like that, too.

"Take your seats, class. I have exciting news." Miss Whistler leaned against her desk and waited for the class to settle down. "We're having Back to School Night on Friday, and the sixth grade is going to do a dance program."

A what? Tully hadn't been listening, but he saw Honey clap her hands together. A very bad sign.

Tully whispered to Ceroy, "What's she talking about?"

"We're going to do a dance program for the parents."

The class buzzed with excitement. Miss Whistler held up her hand for quiet. "We'll let the girls choose their partners."

"Good luck, Tully," said Ceroy. There was a mean gleam in his eyes when he smiled.

For a stunned split second, Tully felt as if he'd been jabbed with an electric cattle prod. He wanted to say something hateful to Ceroy to take the smirk off his face, but his tongue seemed to strangle him.

"We only have five days to practice," Miss Whistler continued, "so Mr. Hubert and I agreed that 'The Bird Dance,' a frisky polka, will be a good choice for our dance number."

Mr. Hubert entered. He looked around the room, and the expression on his moon face changed from enthusiasm to worry. "Unfortunately, we have more girls than boys. Please remember, girls, backstage work is just as important as being in the program."

"I'll do backstage work," Tully volunteered.

"No, Tullis." Mr. Hubert shook his head. "We need every boy on the dance floor."

Miss Whistler was already putting the girls in a line at the front of the class. Mr. Hubert gave Nell papers to pass out with information for the parents about the program. When she handed Tully one, he whispered, "Choose me."

"What?" Nell asked.

"Choose me," he whispered more urgently this time.

Nell smiled the least little bit, then walked off. She probably thought he was a skinny weasel. She probably wanted to choose someone big like Ceroy or someone funny like R.J. He should have spent more time trying to talk to girls so that he'd have some practice when he needed it.

Valerie East chose R.J., and Sissy chose John Ed, and Carrie Ellis chose Ceroy. Honey was next in line. Tully felt as if a freight train were coming right at him. Miss Whistler opened her mouth, but Nell chose that moment to stick the leftover papers in the teacher's hand.

"Oh, thank you, Nell," Miss Whistler said. "You may choose your partner now."

"Tully Webster," Nell said. She threw Tully a quick sideways glance and smiled.

Tully's mouth fell open.

"I'll help backstage," Honey said, looking grimly at Nell.

Ceroy whistled low. "Ooh, boy. I sure wouldn't want to be Nell this week."

Tookie leaned on Tully's desk. "Looks like Nell isn't as afraid of Honey Kotcher as you are, Kissbug."

"Shut up, Tookie," Tully said, but the words nagged at him.

The class rehearsed the program on the stage in the cafeteria, and Tully was surprised at how much fun they had. Couples kept bumping into each other and forgetting where to stop and start. Mr. Hubert would grab Miss Whistler and dance her around to demonstrate. She fussed at him and blushed, but it put her in a good mood and made everyone laugh. Soon they had the dance steps down, and they spent the rest of the week polishing their performance.

Nell was just Tully's size, and she was easy to dance with. At first, Tully was so embarrassed that his ears burned when they jigged around the stage to the corny, old-fashioned music.

"Zigga – zagga – zigga – zagga – hoi – hoi – hoi!" chanted the singer on the record player. Mr. Hubert clapped his hands and jumped about to the beat of the accordion music. Nell just giggled, and soon Tully saw the humor in it, too, and he started having fun.

Best of all, Nell loved hearing about his filly. Every day during rehearsals, she had a new batch of questions for Tully.

"What does she eat? Where does she sleep? How did you decide to name her Valentine?"

Tully had never had a girlfriend, but he found himself thinking about Nell all the time. Then just as he began to feel comfortable, something happened to change it all.

The first few days, Honey had her hands full painting scenery at recess and during dance practice. The backdrop was a beach scene, with moonlight and stars shimmering on the water.

"It's a masterpiece!" Mr. Hubert exclaimed.

"Very realistic." Miss Whistler nodded her approval at Honey.

Honey finished the backdrop Thursday.

During recess, she and Rhoda practiced opening and closing the curtain and starting the polka music on the record player. But throughout the dance practice, Honey just folded her arms and glared at Nell with flinty green eyes. Tully had seen that look before.

12

The night of the program, Tully had an early supper with his mother and Bigun, then he pulled on a clean pair of blue jeans and a white shirt that crackled with starch. Miss Whistler had given the boys red bandannas to stick in their pockets.

It was a dark and star-blown night, and the old school was lit up like a jack-o'-lantern when they drove up in Bigun's truck. Yellow light from the open windows and doors spilled out onto the schoolyard. Mr. Barnes, the principal, greeted parents at the front door.

Tully hurried through the crowds in the halls to the cafeteria. The choir members already had on their robes and were assembling below the stage. The old red velvet curtain was closed, but it rippled and billowed from all the activity behind it.

"Get backstage, Tullis," Mr. Hubert

snapped as he hurried past. "It's time to get ready."

The stage was a flurry of activity. Stars dangled from the ceiling by fishing line, and a big electric fan ruffled the expanse of a blue cellophane ocean. Tully had to admit that Honey's decorations were good.

R.J. had his hair slicked back. He'd also had a haircut, and his ears stuck out. Some of the girls had bright pink patches of makeup on their cheeks and dark mascara on their eyelashes. They were so giddy and breathless that it could have been Christmas morning instead of a balmy night in September.

Tully looked around for Nell.

"Five minutes," Mr. Hubert bellowed. "You all hush back here."

Tully peeked around the curtain. The cafeteria was almost full of parents now, their faces filmed with sweat. Sixteen-ounce hats shifted restlessly from knee to knee. He could see his mother, fanning herself with a program, sitting between Bigun and R.J.'s mother. Tully's stomach fluttered. Where was Nell?

Miss Whistler grabbed his arm and pulled him away from the curtain. Two pink spots blazed on her wrinkled cheeks, and she had Honey in tow.

"Tullis!" she said sharply. "Nell is sick and will be unable to perform in tonight's program. Honey has kindly volunteered to be your partner."

Tully's knees felt like syrup. "She doesn't know the dance," he said, grasping at straws. "And who's going to work the curtains and the record player?"

"Rhoda can do it." Honey smiled. Her hair was fluffed out so that it looked like red cotton balls. "I'd know that dance with my eyes closed," Honey added. She took Tully's wrist and pulled him to the dance formation with the rest of the class.

Nell had been fine all day at school. What kind of sickness could have come on so fast?

The backstage lights blinked off, and there was a scraping of chairs out front as the audience stood up to sing the national anthem with the choir. The big curtains finally parted, and the stage footlights lit up.

"Welcome, welcome," Mr. Barnes boomed into the microphone. "The sixth grade has been working feverishly all week in order to present this program to you. But first our own island treasure, Miss Whistler, will present you with an introduction."

The parents clapped as Miss Whistler went to the microphone at the edge of the stage. She told a mournful story in her crackly voice about a small group of Polish settlers landing in boats on Matagorda Island a long time ago. Most of them had died, but apparently not before they'd done a lot of polka dancing on the beach.

Tully wished he were in Poland—anywhere but on this stage, getting ready to dance with Honey Kotcher. Oh, suck up your guts, he finally told himself. It's only a dance. It won't kill you.

Miss Whistler concluded her story and took an aisle seat in the front row. The music started, and Honey grabbed Tully's hand and flung her arm around his neck. The top of his head just grazed her chin. He circled her waist with his arm, and they bounced with the rest of their classmates in time to the lively music.

Mr. Hubert had taught them a three-step pattern with a skip at the end. At first, Honey stepped with the rest of the class, but after they'd circled the stage once, she got off on the wrong foot and she and Tully lost their place in the circle.

"Whoa now," he whispered. "Which way are we going, here?"

When he tried to guide her back, she shambled around like a confused bear, and he had to take at least three steps to her one just to keep up with her.

There was a tricky point in the dance where the boys were supposed to pivot around the girls, who waited, clapping their hands. Honey stepped out early and danced on ahead of him. Someone in the audience sucked in his breath.

Tully hurried to catch up with her, but he felt like a drowner in a bad dream, trying to take hold of a tree limb. Honey grabbed his arm, but they promptly collided with John Ed and Sissy. Tully stumbled to his knees. The audience broke into gales of raucous laughter. If only the stage would open up and drop him down to China. Mr. Hubert stood in the wings, the stage lights glistening off his scalp, his palms up in despair, and his face beet red as he frantically mouthed, "Get up! Get up!" John Ed and Sissy whirled on past. The rest of the class stared while circling the stage like marbles swirled in a jar.

Tully couldn't move. "Zigga-zagga-zigga-zagga-hoi-hoi-hoi!" chanted the chorus, over and over.

He'd never had trouble with this dance, not even in the very beginning. Let this be a bad dream I wake up from, he prayed as he saw the laughing faces in the audience. An earnest look on her face, Honey suddenly leaned down and picked him up by the waist. His feet skimmed the floor as she danced around with him while he hung on to her.

The audience broke into new fits of laughter. It was too much for Tully. He struggled out of Honey's arms and jerked away from her. The heel of his sneaker snagged in the microphone cord, and he fell heavily again. He caught sight of Miss Whistler. She looked too stunned to move.

Tully scrabbled to his feet. In a dizzying moment—as though all the humiliations of the past year came upon him in a single blow—he pushed his face next to Honey's and yelled, "I hate your guts, you stupid slob!"

Honey caught her breath as if she'd been struck, and tears started in her eyes. Tully ran off the stage and bolted out the stage door, into the warm night.

He ran as fast as he could, but he could still hear the accelerating music as it gushed out the open windows of the auditorium.

"Ziggazaggaziggazaggahoihoihoi! Ziggazaggaziggazaggahoihoihoi!" over and over, like a war chant.

Rhoda caught up with him at the end of the parking lot.

"Nell was too scared to come. Honey threatened her in the bathroom after school." Rhoda's breathless voice shook by Tully's side as she ran to keep up. "She told her, 'If you tell anyone, you'll be sorry.' "

Shame slammed into him in waves. It was bad enough that he'd put Dane in Honey's path so that he could avoid her, but this was worse: to hide behind Nell!

Rhoda dropped back. Tully's side hurt, but he kept running, past the Island Store and across the village square. When he reached the road to the ranch, rifts of quicksilver from the moonlight shone out of the clouds to light his way.

Once in the house, Tully found his class list in a kitchen drawer and dialed Nell's number with a shaking hand. While her telephone rang, he twined the cord nervously between his fingers.

Tully recognized Nell's voice when she answered. "I know what Honey Kotcher did, and it's all my fault," Tully said, his voice unsteady. "If I hadn't asked you to choose me, it never would have happened. I'm sorry."

There was only silence on the other end.

"Are you all right?" Tully asked.

"I'm okay," Nell said in a small voice. "And, Tully?"

"Yeah?"

"I would have chosen you anyway."

Tully felt his way upstairs. He turned on the light over the sink in the bathroom and splashed cold water on his face. He saw himself in the mirror, and a scared, skinny chicken stared back at him. Well, that's what I am, Tully thought.

He pulled his clothes off in the dark of his room. Lying on top of the covers, he stared out the window at the yard trees. Every time he tried to close his eyes, he saw Honey looming over him while he stumbled, and a hundred different laughs echoed in his head. Somehow worse than that was the memory of Honey's stricken face and her tears. He'd yelled at her in front of everyone.

He heard Bigun's truck rattle over the pipes of the cattle guard. Then Bigun's heavy footsteps on the moaning stair boards, followed by his mother's lighter ones.

Bigun sat down on Tully's bed, his hands dangling between his knees. Tully saw his mother's silhouette in the doorway.

"I guess your dance partner tonight was the

gal you told me about that night in the barn, the one that was pesterin' you?" Bigun asked.

Tully turned his face away when the tears pooled in his eyes.

"I know her daddy," Bigun continued. "He used to be a fisherman, but most of the time now he does nothing in particular, and he doesn't even do that very well. There's lots of no-good in that man, Tully. It can't be easy living with him."

Tully's feelings were a-jumble. "Don't you think I know that? But you don't know what all she's done to me," Tully shouted. "She didn't just ruin the program tonight; she's ruined my life. I can't ever show my face at school again."

"It just seems that way right now, Tully," his mother said. "By Monday morning, you'll feel differently."

"Leave me be," Tully said, as he felt the tightness break in his throat. He turned on his stomach and put his face in the pillow.

When Tully woke in the night, he was lying on his side, one arm numb under the weight of his head. He twisted in the sheet, pushing back against his memory of the program. At first he thought a ringtail had screamed or a coyote howled. After he lay listening for a while, he knew it wasn't a sound that had awakened him, but a feeling.

He was nobody's hero, that was for sure. But he wasn't afraid of Honey Kotcher anymore.

13

R.J. came over early Monday morning.

"Thought I'd better come get you or you might not go to school," R.J. said as they started out. The shadow of a buzzard skated on the road in front of them.

"I'm not afraid of her anymore," Tully said. "She can beat me up if she wants to, but I won't be scared of her again."

R.J. pulled a weed and chewed it, eyeing him sidewise. "*I'm* scared of her. Remember that time in the third grade when I brought my conch shell to school for show-and-tell?"

"Yeah," Tully said. "She busted it to smithereens after school. I wanted to help you, but I didn't."

R.J.'s fine yellow hair went every which way in the wind. "She would have knocked the bejesus out of you," R.J. said.

Tully saw Honey in front of the school. She was sitting on a bench under the flagpole, holding something in her lap. He was on the top step when she ran up after him and thrust an open box into his hands.

"Here, Tully," she said breathlessly. "I'm giving this to you."

A small horned toad lay on a bed of cotton. It had bright spots and horny spikes all over its back and two small horns on its head. Because he was supposed to be so old, Honey had named the horned toad Rip, after Rip Van Winkle. Tully remembered her playing with him in the sand during recess in the first grade. She'd bring an empty sardine can to school and hitch him up to it with string, and he'd pull it like a wagon. Mrs. Fuller, their second-grade teacher, had let Rip live on the windowsill by Honey's desk all year. She said it was because Rip was such a good fly catcher, but Tully knew that Mrs. Fuller felt sorry for Honey because her father wouldn't let her have dogs and cats or birds and fish like the other kids. Aside from the baby alligators last summer, Rip was the only pet Honey had ever had.

"I don't want it." Tully shoved the box back at Honey.

"Keep it, Tully," Honey said. "It's special. I want you to have it."

"I don't want anything of yours." Tully looked around and saw R.J. and Ceroy and John Ed, their eyes wide, at the bottom of the steps. Tookie and Rhoda and Sissy were hovering and bobbing on the sidewalk like a flock of curious birds.

Tully reminded himself that he wasn't afraid of Honey anymore. What would a person who wasn't scared do?

"Leave me alone," Tully said fiercely, and turned to go into the building.

"Wait, Tully," Honey said as she took his arm. Without thinking, Tully put the palm of his hand on her face and pushed as hard as he could. Honey stumbled backward down the steps and landed hard on her bottom. But for her freckles, she was as white as the face of an apple half.

"Don't bother me anymore," Tully yelled.

He strode down the hall, with R.J. hurrying to catch up with him.

"She's going to get you, Tully."

They passed Honey's Kissbug poster on the

127

wall, and Tully yanked it down and left it on the floor.

"I don't care," Tully said, more reckless than he felt.

When Honey took her seat at the back of the room, the class was hushed and tense. Tully's words seemed to have taken the starch out of her. She sat by herself at lunch, and during recess she perched on a punk log and drew pictures in the dirt with a stick.

Everyone but R.J. shied away from Tully all day. He figured that no one wanted to be with him when Honey decided to get even. Just before school let out that afternoon, Miss Whistler called Tully and Honey into the hall.

"What happened on Friday night was unfortunate," Miss Whistler said, looking at Honey with eyes as brown and warm as a butternut. "Honey, I wish you'd admitted that you didn't know the dance."

Honey said nothing; she miserably watched her toes.

Miss Whistler clucked her tongue against the roof of her mouth. "What's done is done, though, and we can't change it now. There will be no more said of it; and we must simply put it behind us."

On Tuesday afternoon, John Ed threw up in the wastebasket, and Miss Whistler left to take him to the nurse's office. Honey dropped a note on Tully's desk, but when she turned to go back to her seat, Ceroy stuck his foot out and she pitched forward on the floor with a splat. Tully shredded the note.

Everyone waited for Honey to lunge at Ceroy or tell him that she'd get him after school, but she didn't. She just went back to her seat and sat there as though she were frozen.

Tully heard Carrie's angry half-whisper. "She deserves it. She ruined the whole program."

"She cut my braid off in the second grade," Sissy said in a quiet voice.

"She scared Nell into staying home Friday night, too," Rhoda said.

The class looked at Nell, but she turned away and opened her library book.

The next day, during math, Miss Whistler was at the blackboard, her voice punctuated by squeaking chalk.

"Sail frog," John Ed suddenly chirped, and he flipped a dried-out, squashed frog across the room like a Frisbee. It hit Honey square in the mouth.

A wave of laughter washed over the room, while John Ed smirked at Honey from the safety of his desk. When Miss Whistler's eyes darted around the room, Honey wiped her face with her sleeve, but otherwise she appeared as if nothing had happened.

At the end of the week, during social studies, Miss Whistler pulled down the roll-up map of Europe. Someone had taped a large sheet of paper over it. It read:

HIP HIP HOORAY!!
HONEY KOTCHER IS GOING AWAY!!

Just below the writing was a crude drawing of Honey waving good-bye from the back of a boat.

"Great Jehosephat!" Miss Whistler paled visibly, clinging to the chalk trough for support. She tore off the paper and threw it in the wastebasket.

For a moment, Tully wondered if Honey actually *was* moving away. Then he saw Carrie and Sissy exchange glances, and he knew it was their joke. R.J. turned his face to the side and covered a burst of laughter by forcing a coughing fit.

One by one, everyone who had ever been skunked by Honey found a way to get back at her. Tully kept waiting for her to lash out, but she just sat at her desk, squashed into herself. She looked at Tully only when she had to now, and it wasn't a hard look or a soft one. Something in her face reminded Tully of a house where no one is home, or even expected home. Yet not to be picked on or to be the object of Honey's attention was better than any gift he could imagine. Whenever it bothered him to see the other kids humiliate Honey, he tried to remind himself that she was getting a taste of her own medicine.

One afternoon, Miss Whistler sent Honey on an errand to the office. After the door was shut, the teacher stood in front of her desk.

"It's obvious that Honey has become the target of a hate campaign. Mind you, she's never complained to me, but I have eyes. These old ears may take longer to put things together than they used to, but they eventually put things together quite well."

"She deserves it," Sissy cried.

"She's sure picked on us enough," R.J. said.

"Yeah, what about all the things *she's* done?" Tookie said.

"No one deserves *this*," said Miss Whistler in her deliberate tones, slashing the air with a flat palm. "To be badly treated by one classmate is difficult, I'll hand you that. But to be the brunt of *all* your classmates' anger? Well, that's something else again."

Tully's face burned. He knew she was right, but what could *he* do about it?

14

The days went by. The sea winds became cooler, and the fog rolled in during the night and wound itself around the clattering palm trees. Fall was on the way. Even the ocean looked softer and bluer.

One morning in October, Tully stood behind Rhoda while they waited to turn in their English homework. He glanced over her shoulder and saw the title of her essay: "Why I Hate Miss Whistler."

Tully's heart pinwheeled. Why would Rhoda, the most timid little mouse he knew, admit to Miss Whistler in writing that she hated her? He strained to read some of the essay, but the writing was scrawled and messy, not at all like Rhoda's usually perfect handwriting. It didn't make sense.

Honey put her paper on the top of the stack, then Nell moved forward and turned in her essay. Rhoda stepped up behind Nell and quickly drew out Honey's essay and substituted the one she was holding. Tully saw "Honey Kotcher" scrawled on the top of the page, with the date under it. Rhoda then slipped a neatly written essay titled "Why I Don't Eat Meat," by Rhoda Webb, on the top of the stack. As she passed Tully, Rhoda balled up Honey's paper and threw it in the wastebasket.

Miss Whistler graded the essays the next day while the class was doing math work sheets. It had been a long, draggy afternoon, and Tully felt drowsy in the stuffy classroom. He wanted to put his head down for a snooze, and he glanced up at Miss Whistler to see if she'd notice. Just then she blinked and caught her breath, and her thin, ropy hands flew to her throat. Was she was reading the phony essay?

Honey was bent over her work sheet, the box with the horned toad nestled in her lap. She'd always seemed as alert as a nervous horse, but lately she looked more hollow-eyed.

Miss Whistler folded the paper and slipped it into her pocket. She walked to Honey's desk and quietly said, "I'd like to speak with you outside, please."

Tully saw Honey quietly slip the box with the horned toad into her desk. She pushed herself up from the chair. Head down, arms moving stiffly at her sides, she scuffed out behind Miss Whistler.

Tully was flooded with pity for Honey, and he hated the feeling. She'd made him miserable. Sissy was right. She deserved all this and more. So why did he care?

Ceroy ran to Honey's desk and drew the box out. He dangled the horned toad aloft for the whole room to see, a big-shot grin on his face. When they heard Miss Whistler's shuffle coming down the hall, Ceroy thrust the box inside his desk.

Honey stayed out of class for the rest of the day. During recess, Ceroy slipped the horned toad into his shirt pocket, and followed by the class, he searched outside, behind the building, for a hiding place.

Taking Rip out of his pocket, Ceroy stroked his belly in the glary sunshine. Rhoda spied a rusty iron cover on the ground. She lifted it up and saw that it was a lid for the school's water meter. Red ants and doodlebugs scattered on the cool wet ground.

"This is a regular horny toad restaurant, Rip," Ceroy said. He put Rip on the ground and replaced the cover.

Just before school let out, Honey came back to the room to get her books. She stacked them, then looked inside her desk. A frantic expression came over her face, and she pushed her chair back and got down on her knees, pulling papers and notebooks and pens out onto the floor. The bell rang and the class filed out, while Honey sat on the floor in a heap, with a miserable look in her eyes.

Tully was out in the schoolyard with R.J. and Rhoda and Nell when Honey ran up to him.

"No one else will tell me." Honey's red-rimmed eyes were huge, and she touched his sleeve with freckled fingers. "Do you know where Rip is?"

"Why would I know about your ol' horned toad?" Tully asked.

"I put him in my desk, and now he's gone." Tears streamed down her face. "I've had him almost all my life. It's not fair for somethin' bad to happen to Rip because everybody hates *me*."

Tully was shocked. R.J.'s mouth hung open, while Rhoda blinked and Nell kicked at the dirt. They were stunned to see that this girl, who had made everyone else cry, could cry herself.

"He's mine," she said, her voice raw. "You didn't want him. If you know where he is, please tell me."

"I don't know what you're talking about," Tully said, and walked away.

Tully lay in bed that night and tried to erase his mind like a blackboard, but Honey Kotcher's tear-streaked face kept appearing. He finally went out to the barn, where the horses stamped and blew in their stalls, and the air was thick with the ripe, familiar smell of manure and dusty hay. He lit a Coleman lantern and hung it on a nail outside Risky's stall. Risky's tail switched quickly, and she turned her face back to look at him in the sooty shadows. Tully walked in beside her, talking and running his hand along her hide. The muscles of her jaws bunched, and she blinked at him.

He spread a horse blanket over the straw in a corner of the stall. The tree frogs and night crickets shrilled outside in the brush. They made such a steady racket that Tully stopped hearing it after a while and watched Risky munch her oats.

After a time, he heard footsteps. "I thought I saw a light out here," Red said, and leaned against the stall. His hands capped the top of the door, and he rested his chin on them.

Tully took a deep breath and tried to find the right words in a jumble of false starts. "Have you ever hated someone so much that you wanted awful things to happen to them, but when they did, you felt bad?"

"Sure," Red said.

Tully felt so relieved that the whole story just came pouring out. He told Red how Honey had badgered him last year and how she'd loved him this year and made things worse than ever. When he told him about Coffin Creek and the dance program, Red laughed and his face cracked into a net of shallow lines. The story just kept spilling out until Tully finally told him about all the things they'd done to Honey to get even.

"When I saw how much she missed that ol' horny toad today, I just felt bad, that's all," Tully said. "She ain't got much that's worth wanting."

"Maybe you're ready to forgive her," Red said. "Remember when you got tired of hating Risky?"

"But it's not so hard to forgive something you love," Tully said. "How do you forgive someone you hate?"

"There ain't nothin' in life that squares up neat and tidy at the corners, Tully." Red broke a long stalk of hay into small pieces. "There's those that can hate forever, but what they really hate is their ownselves. Sooner or later the rest of us just have to give it up in order to go on looking ourselves in the mirror every day."

When Tully woke in the morning, he still

wasn't sure that Red was right. After all, Red had never met Honey Kotcher. But Tully knew that he couldn't keep Rip hidden from her. He dressed early and got to school just as the janitor drove up in his truck. Tully took a box from his backpack and went behind the building to the rusty meter lid. When he lifted it, Rip blinked up at him.

Tully put the box in Honey's desk and sat down at his own desk to do the homework he hadn't gotten around to.

Just before lunch, Honey was behind Tully at the pencil sharpener.

"I know it was you that gave Rip back," she whispered.

Tully smiled and took his seat.

At recess, R.J. got a ball from the closet and called a dodgeball game by the side of the building. Honey was on the punk log, holding Rip.

"You're It, Tookie," R.J. said.

"I ain't," Tookie said. "It's John Ed's turn to be It."

"I was It first yesterday," John Ed said. "What about Ceroy?"

"Tully ought to be It just for givin' Honey that horned toad back." Ceroy glared at Tully and threw the ball at him.

Tully fiddled with his belt buckle and kicked his boot heel in the dirt. His heart began hammering as if he were about to do something brave.

"Rip belongs to Honey," Tully finally said. "Honey's finished pickin' on us, and we're finished pickin' on her."

He waited for someone to say something sarcastic, but they just looked at Honey.

"Then Honey can be It," John Ed finally said.

Tully breathed a sigh of relief. "You want to play dodgeball, Honey?"

Honey got off the punk log and dropped Rip in her shirt pocket. She shrugged and put a blank look on her face, but Tully noticed that she walked straighter. "Sure, I'll be It," she said, and caught the ball Tully threw to her.

Dona Schenker is the author of *Throw a Hungry Loop,* which won a Spur Award from the Western Writers of America and was a finalist in the Texas Lone Star Reading List. A Texas native and former librarian, she is the author of many short stories for young people. *Fearsome's Hero* is her second novel. She lives with her husband and two sons in San Antonio.